THOSE WE SEEK

MARIE JONES

Copyright © 2023 by Marie Jones

Cover Designer: Fiona Suherman

Supervising Editor: Shannon Marks

Editing Assistants: Kristen Scheaffer, and Cheyenne Main

Publishing Assistant: Lisa Wood

Paperback ISBN: 978-1-958503-35-5

Hardback ISBN: 978-1-958503-36-2

All rights reserved.

No part of this book may be reproduced in any form or by any electronic or
mechanical means, including information storage and retrieval systems,
without written permission from the author, except for the use of brief
quotations in a book review.

THOSE WE SEEK

sequel to *Those We Trust*
by **Marie Jones**

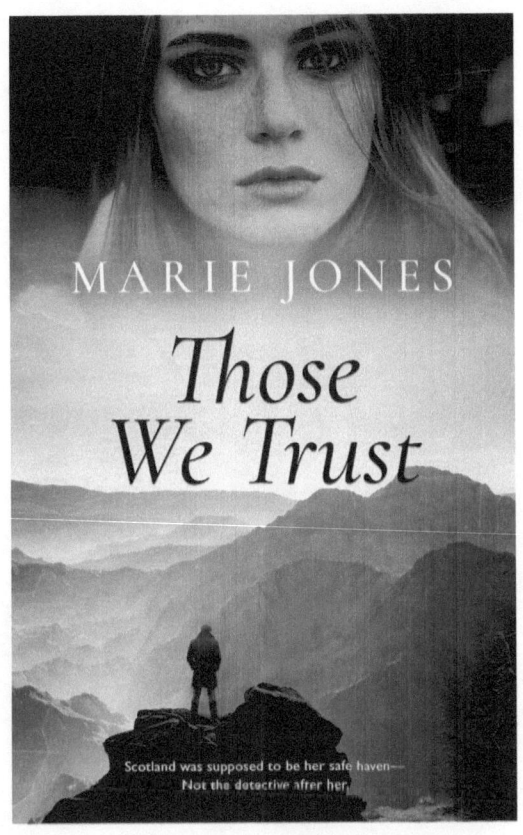

To my husband, Nigel, and my family, who loves and supports me
To my daughter, Emily, my fantastic book plotter and reader
To my son, Luke, my fabulous encourager

In loving memory of my mum-in-law, Rosemary,
who loved nothing more than to sit and enjoy a good book

To my number one wonderful fan, Betty

'Feitheamh rium, feitheamh rium, mo leannan
leig dhomh d 'aghaidh fhaicinn ann an solas na grèine.
ruighinn a-mach agus grèim orm
Agus tilg air falbh faileas na h-oidhche.'
Scottish Gaelic

'Wait for me, wait for me, my beloved
Let me see your face in the sunlight.
Reach out and touch me
And cast away the shadows of the night.'
English translation

Sometimes the sun touches your skin,
casting out the shadows and bringing you warmth.
Other times stormy clouds will come to eclipse its light,
leaving you shivering in its wake.
The rise and fall of the sun is never in our control,
It's not for us to demand and restrain.
But we can capture every sunrise revealed in its glory
... until the day it stops rising for us.

I thought the darkness could no longer touch me.
I was wrong.

PROLOGUE

The cold, sharp wind whipped against my numb cheeks, stinging my eyes, and causing me to inhale rapidly. The uneven rocks beneath my feet made me stumble and curse. My legs, aching from the frantic steep climb, moaned as I forced them on. My heart beat too fast, like fluttering wings of an insect desperate to escape its trap.

Yet I had to keep going. *I must.* His life, the only one I cared desperately about, rested solely on me. So, I would keep climbing, until there was nowhere further to go, and the light lost its battle against the gathering darkness.

All I could see in my mind was him, the last look he'd given me. Long now I'd realised I only felt strong with him by my side. But he wouldn't believe that now. I'd done my job too well, too effectively. The memory of my parting words had me choking back a suffocating cry. No, this time I was truly alone. Alone, except for an enemy waiting for me — surrounding me from all sides. And this enemy wanted my blood. Nothing else would satisfy.

As if I'd conjured up the voice from my darkest terrors,

seeping coldly into my skin, the wind taunted, "You better keep climbing if you want to reach him in time."

I spun around, trying to peer through the descending clouds, as if to see how close on my heels they were. I could just make out the dim shadow of a moving person. Fear ripped through me.

I had no choice but to keep climbing. We both knew that. Something more powerful than me had me scrambling up once more on my hands and knees, barely feeling the stones cutting into my skin.

I should have known this wasn't over. What a stupid fool I was to believe our love would shelter us from danger. That it would act as a shield against the enemies lurking in the shadows, turning us from predators into prey.

The darkness was coming for us.

It was coming for me.

[1]

EIGHT WEEKS EARLIER

I stretched out luxuriously, a lazy smile on my face. The sunrays, not yet warm in the Scottish sky but welcomed nonetheless, danced over our skin where we lay. I heard a distant birdsong and, if I listened carefully, the soft rippling of the loch.

I was in the only place I ever truly felt safe, and at peace: in the warmth of our bed, with my husband lying beside me.

After facing death six months ago, I adopted this strange little ritual each morning to convince myself I was here, that this man I loved was beside me and I'd never have to wake up without him. I would raise myself onto my elbow and drink Marcus in as he lay sleeping, half on his stomach and half on his side, with one arm stretched out towards me. His mouth slightly open with that hint of a smile that drove me crazy with longing. His smooth skin asking to be touched.

I couldn't resist, like most mornings, from reaching out and stroking back his brown waves, stirring him from his slumber with a soft grunt of protest.

One of his blue-green eyes reluctantly opened, squinting against the brightness of the light before focusing on my grinning face.

"Did I wake you?" I innocently asked, then laughed as he pulled me down against him.

"As good as it feels when you touch me, could you have not waited until I'm fully conscious before doing so?" he mumbled, closing his eyes again as if preparing to go back to sleep, naively thinking he had me in a position to keep still.

Ah, the poor innocent boy. Where there's a will, there's a way...

When my rather cold feet just happened to touch his warm legs, Marcus yelped, eyes flying wide open. I snorted, only to give a small laughing scream as he flipped me over, trapping me beneath him.

"Ah, I see you're full of trouble this morning, *mo leannan*. Looking for something from your poor unsuspecting husband?" His eyes held their own mischievous trouble as he gazed down at me with that hint of a smile.

An inviting smile danced across my lips, encouraging him to press down onto me so I could feel his skin against mine. As our lips met, I felt the all-too-familiar pain in my side and involuntarily flinched. Marcus immediately pulled back. His fingertips gently touched the scar on my side, still tender and sore after all this time.

"I'm sorry, I should be more care—"

I immediately cut him off, touching his lips with my own fingers. "No, no, you're not hurting me, I promise." Then, before he could protest further and move off me, I was drawing him back into a kiss, stroking his back and over his ass, then around to cup him in a way I knew drove him crazy.

"Oh, you play dirty, Mrs. Armstrong," he murmured, before moving his lips down my body, lingering over my breasts, setting my skin alight and pushing the pain far away. Together, we found the rhythm of our bodies and as he moved inside me, I felt the explosion of pure joy that few know. And I thanked God for it.

A WHILE LATER, we ate hot porridge on the veranda overlooking the loch. The morning was still chilly in the crisp September air, so I wrapped a tartan blanket around me, enjoying its comforting warmth. We had been chatting companionably, but I sensed Marcus begin to withdraw from me as his mind turned to work.

Though he was careful not to break any professional rules with case details, he often sought me out for my advice, especially when he was feeling frustrated. That is, except the one where I was the main survivor, my ex-husband still at large, and the fraud ring still unbroken. The one that kept my husband restless at night and consumed him by day as it remained unsolved. And the one he wouldn't share with me, though I yearned for him to. I needed that closure, desperately.

I also needed to stop feeling so damn afraid and anxious. My newfound confidence of a few months ago had taken a bleak turn with the betrayal of both my best friend, Ella, and my ex-husband, Richard. It had turned out that I was worth nothing to them, simply a pawn to be used for their own gain. They were too consumed with themselves and their selfish desires to have ever cared about anyone, least of all me. Somehow, though the words begged to be released, I had kept these feelings from Marcus. I knew he would understand, would reassure me, and tell me how much he loved me and strive to make me feel better. I loved him for it, but this crushing self-doubt felt like my failure, a battle *I* needed to overcome to bring back the strong woman I was becoming before the attack – before it all went to shit. So, I didn't tell him of the nightmares that had been consuming me in a cold sweat the last few nights —Richard, eyes glinting wildly with murder, his cold laughter echoing as he advanced towards me with that sharp, steel knife aimed directly at my heart, and me unable to scream or move. All it would do was make Marcus feel even more driven to work all hours to hunt him down and add another layer of unnecessary guilt that he hadn't apprehended Richard while I'd lain there bleeding in his arms.

But I should have guessed Marcus, ever the detective, had sensed something was wrong. He turned to me now and gave me one of those intense looks of his as he casually said, "You were a wee bit restless last night."

So much for concealing it. "Just... dreams."

He reached out and took my hand. "Ach, they sounded a little more than dreams." His gaze grew more intense, and I felt myself flush. "I thought I heard you say Richard's name."

What could I say to that? We held firmly to the promise of always speaking the truth. But if he knew the extent, that I was falling apart inside... I replied as nonchalantly as I could, "Oh, you know, just my old nightmare that comes every once in a while... when I... see him, standing there."

Hi eyes held mine intently, fiercely. "You've got nothing to be afraid of, mo leannan. He won't come back here or harm you again, I swear it."

To take away the deep frown of concern creasing his forehead, I reached up and touched his cheek. "I know. I always feel safe when I'm with you," I smiled, kissing him gently.

He pulled me into a tight embrace, pressing me against

him, before reluctantly letting go. "I should get to the station."

"Guess that means I should get on with work too." I pulled a face. To my relief, Marcus chuckled.

We collected the breakfast dishes and made our way inside. Marcus walked over to the kitchen sink to wash out the bowls. If I was going to say anything, I needed to do it now. I inhaled a breath then blurted out, "How's the case going... in finding him?"

I watched him go still. Keeping his back to me, he softly replied, "You know I can't talk about it."

I felt a bit of indignation mixed with frustration. "Since when has that ever stopped you?"

He turned with faint smile, seeing me with my arms crossed, eyebrows raised. I glared at him but dropped my arms. In a quieter voice, I muttered, "What aren't you telling me? You're holding something back. I can sense it."

There was a moment of stillness as Marcus weighed my words. He came towards me and cupped his hands around my face. I felt him kiss my forehead before resting his head against mine. "I'll tell you soon, I promise. Just trust me."

I sighed softly. "You know I do. I always will." *But I need to know soon.*

[2]

The station was already buzzing with activity when Marcus walked in. After having been held up by roadworks on the way into Inverness, he was running later than he planned. He gave a couple of colleagues a nod as he passed through the bull pit area to reach his compact office, where he shut the door with relief.

His head swirled with thoughts, his shoulders tense and painful. The utter joy and release he felt whenever he was with Sophia, alone in bed and their home, already felt like a distant dream. And he knew why – the strain of keeping so much back from her when he wanted nothing more than to share with her burdened him. "But I'm doing the right thing," Marcus muttered to himself. "I won't let her keep reliving it." The nightmares she was experiencing clearly haunted her, though she tried to play them down. The crying out of her ex's name as she tossed and moaned in her sleep, he didn't dare dwell on. Old jealousy could all too easily creep up on him as it had before. It was bad enough that he had to deal with the guilt of not protecting her when she needed him the most—

No. The only thing that mattered, the only thing he could do, was to bring in not only Richard, but the criminals who'd masterminded this whole damn fraud ring. And that's what he was going to do, even if it killed him.

Marcus spread out the file in front of him, once again trying to piece together the facts and spot anything he might have missed. Discovering that Sophia's computer codes from a programme she had created were being used to commit fraud should have stopped this nice little ring from continuing. After all, Aneella, Sophia's old university friend who'd stolen them for Richard, had been apprehended and was going to court any day now. But she had only been a pawn in a clever, dangerous crime that was gripping his country. Every time they thought they were close to getting to the source of the accounts, somehow this account would mysteriously close, and the process would have to start again. It was clear someone was informing them whenever Marcus and his team were about to strike. And it was frustrating as hell.

That was why Richard had to be found and brought in. He was their only link to them. Lyle, who had been an accomplice before his use had come to an end, had nothing to offer them now. They needed to pin this bastard down.

The door to his office swung open. His new Detective Sergeant, Tom Edgings, ambled in, smiling confidently as the youngsters always did. Marcus gave him a raised eyebrow and a faint smile. In truth, he liked Tom. He reminded him of his younger, eager self. And with Tom's arrival came the departure of his old DS, Morven — and that had been the best bit of news he'd had in a very long time. Let's just say he may have 'encouraged' her back to Glasgow by handing her an approved transfer request she hadn't even seen. When her crush on him turned sour as his relationship with Sophia evolved, he was more than eager to see her leave. At least there was no worries about that with Tom—he was as much of an alpha male as it was possible to get.

"Alright, boss?" Tom said now, whistling a little under his breath. "What criminals are we catching today then?"

"Tom, remember: it's 'sir,' not 'boss,'" Marcus remarked in his mild tone. "Save boss for the future Mrs. Edgings. God help her, whoever she may be."

Tom tried to look offended but ended up chuckling as he protruded out his chest with the presentation of a proud peacock. "Me, marry some wee lass? And deprive the women of Inverness of this muscular body? I couldn't do that; it just wouldn't be fair."

Marcus took in Tom's slim frame and bit his lip to stop from snorting with laughter. "No, no, quite right, mustn't deprive them of such a fine specimen of manhood. Any chance this male perfection could update me on where we've got to in the Browning case?" he continued as he moved around to lean on the desk, his eyes intent on his sergeant.

Tom was quick to take the hint and updated Marcus with his first case he had been leading on, finishing with, "With Browning in custody here, and enough evidence to wallpaper the cell he is currently enjoying in our hospitality, he will soon be confessing to the theft of his business partner's riches, no sweat."

"Good, good." Marcus nodded, reading over the case file. He looked up and grinned. "Excellent work, Sergeant." He held the file out to Tom.

Tom bolstered at this praise and took the case documents with a huge grin plastered across his face. "Thank you, boss-sir! And I'm ready for more responsibility. What do you want me to take on next?"

In answer, Marcus scrutinised Tom to the point his

sergeant began to look a little warm under his crumpled shirt.

"Tom, I'm going to bring you into a case that's extremely personal to me. One that requires your utmost discretion and commitment. Can I trust you in that?"

Tom nodded his head vigorously. "Aye, absolutely!"

Something in his eager face reassured Marcus more than any words could. He nodded, then indicated to Tom to take a seat before sitting himself.

"Good... because I need your discretion. This case involves an attack on the person who matters the most to me – my wife, Sophia." His voice caught as he said her name. He took a breath before continuing with a voice laced with steel, "And believe me when I say, you and I will not give up until the bastard and his accomplices are caught."

THE STEAMING cup of tea in my hands soothed me as I sat staring out of my window, mustering up the motivation I needed to finish this computer program. I was due to meet my client, an up-and-coming PR company based in Edinburgh, this afternoon to show them the first draft of their programme, which would assist them in producing a linked approach to all their media platforms. Right now, it was looking a little rough, even for a first draft. Actually, "rough" was being complimentary.

Sighing, I reluctantly put my mug down and turned back around to the desk Marcus had made for me to avoid becoming distracted by the gorgeous vista. Telling myself that the loch or distant munro mountain wasn't going anywhere, I settled down and grimly got on with the task at hand.

That was, until an email flashed across my screen.

Everything in me stilled. My heart leapt erratically.

In disbelief, I stared at the words until they began to swim and blur before me.

Sender: (*Hidden from recipient*)

Subject: Read this

I'm sorry. There, I've said it.

Now you're going to help me.

Don't let me down.

I FELT like I'd been dealt a paralysing blow. I fought to catch my breath. I thought I'd felt fear before, but now I realised that there was a more dangerous kind of fear—the kind that floored you, and made you feel as though you were being watched.

Richard.

I pushed back on the chair, scraping the legs against the floor to distance myself from the computer, from *it*. My hand moved to hover over my scar. I could still feel the cold steel plunging into my side, the searing pain following in its path. A sob escaped me, swiftly followed by bile. Hand over mouth, I rushed over to the sink and leaned over, heaving.

When the sickness abated, I grabbed a glass and filled it with water, slowly sipping the liquid, squeezing my eyes shut. *Calm down, you have to calm down. Think. Think!*

My instinct was to call Marcus. My hand was already reaching for my phone: I wanted to hear his warm, reassuring voice. Yet as I went to dial, something caused me to pause, my hand to freeze. I needed to clear the fog lurking in my brain and think this through. As soon as Marcus saw this email, I knew he would trace the IP address, try to find where it was sent from. But if Richard guessed this, he would cut contact and disappear once more... and maybe never be found. Or worse, I would never get closure.

But if I played along, tried to find out more information as to where he was hiding, then maybe I could entice him out into the open. Then, and only then, I could tell Marcus so that together we could bring him in. Then we would finally be free.

My plan carried a huge risk. I wasn't stupid. Any love Richard may have felt for me once was long gone. He still wanted those computer codes, still had dangerous men chasing him who therefore would also be chasing me. And that was why I couldn't let my husband know—there was no way he would ever let me become live bait.

Bait.

Vulnerable. Exposed.

The thought pushed me over the edge. I pushed through the front door and broke into a run, not stopping until I reached the calm waters of the loch. I crouched down to stare into the clear surface, willing it to give me the strength I needed. I saw my pale, scared face reflected at me. I moved my hand over the water to dispel it, not wanting to see my eyes until they were filled with strength and resolve.

Somewhere within me I must find the courage again.

For Marcus.

For me. So I could feel whole again.

[3]

Cathy paced the threadbare carpet, anxiously biting her lip. Her daughter's letter lay in her hands, a little crushed beneath tense hands. Checking on her husband, Derek, in the front room they'd converted to a bedroom, she heard his soft breathing, the only sound that she ever heard from him. Each day he slipped a little further away from her. For one sharp, bittersweet moment she yearned for his stroke never to have happened, if only so that she could share this with him and ease this excruciating pressure on her. She didn't want to carry this alone.

With a choked back cry, Cathy continued her pacing. Back and forth. Back and forth. Her heart felt broken. How could her own daughter, her beloved daughter, do such a thing to her friend?

Nothing in this world made sense to her now, her little world she had so carefully nurtured and protected was crumbling around her. How could she ever make it all better again?

IT WAS dark when I eventually arrived home from my client's meeting in Edinburgh. I normally loved visiting the city, sometimes with Marcus. I often lingered on the castle grounds and in the characteristic shops, enjoying the nostalgic warmth, occasionally staying overnight if I could afford to. But tonight, I wanted to get back to our lodge and feel safe in Marcus' arms, under his soothing touch.

I dropped my bag just inside the door and smiled as I heard the familiar sound of whistling coming from the kitchen. Marcus was stirring chicken and vegetables in a frying pan. The worktops were covered in various utensils and ends of peppers, courgettes, and all manner of our kitchen utensils. My initial welcome smile turned to a wide grin as I came up behind him, putting my arms around his waist.

"I see you're creating a culinary masterpiece that requires items I had no idea we possessed."

Marcus, startled by my sudden appearance, jerked the hand holding the spatula. We watched as a piece of chicken soared through the air in spectacular fashion and landed on the worktop, amidst the abandoned vegetable ends.

"Oops," I laughed, kissing him on the cheek as he turned towards me.

"Your fault, lass. I hope you feel suitably bad knowing that piece of chicken will never be enjoyed by our fine taste buds."

"I'm mourning it right now. Perhaps we should conduct a funeral for it."

Marcus laughed softly, "And have a wee toast in its memory. And as it happens..."

He reached across for a glass of scotch whisky sitting nearby and raised it to the chicken sitting forlorn in the pan. "Slainte and thank you for your sacrifice, my fine warrior."

With that Marcus took a large gulp, then turned in my arms to pass the glass to me. I took a sip, grimacing a little, then shook my head.

"You are off your rocker, you know that, right?" I commented mildly.

"Mmm," he murmured, before bending to kiss me.

The frying pan made an alarming hiss of protest. We broke apart and stared down into the frying pan. The chicken and vegetables sat there, looking sad and charcoaled.

He frowned hard. "I'm thinking it might need a Marcus special touch."

I raised my eyebrows. "Well, it certainly needs something! Slightly starving wife here..."

"Never fear, mo leannan, your husband can rescue this." With that, Marcus chucked the last of the whisky straight into the frying pan before I could stop him.

"No!" I exclaimed.

The flames that erupted were rather impressive, it had to be said.

But that didn't mean we didn't both give a girlie scream in blind panic before Marcus had the sense to turn off the heat while I rushed to get a wet towel to throw over the pan.

The flame disappeared to a pitiful smoke, leaving behind what once was considered chicken and vegetables but now was nothing more than lumps of coal. We both stood there, breathing hard. Then I turned and pointed a threatening finger at him, my eyes dancing with my own dangerous flames. He gulped and sensibly took a step back.

"You will never do that 'Marcus special' again or it won't be the chicken having a funeral! You hearing me?"

Marcus stared at me. "Okay, you're a wee bit scary right now."

I glared at him, taking a step closer. "That's because I've driven six hours today, had no lunch and my dinner has now gone up in flames, literally! You know precisely what I'm like when I'm hungry."

Silence. Then, "Think I'm going to call for takeout. Sure, deliveroo delivers this far out...please god." Marcus was already curving his way around me to a safe distance away and reaching for his mobile.

My eyes narrowed. "It had better, DI Armstrong. It had better."

"FEELING BETTER?"

Marcus was eyeing me rather cautiously over the remains of our Chinese takeaway. I sat back, rubbing my full tummy, torn between keeping up my image as a dangerous woman to cross and laughing outright.

I didn't have the energy to keep the pretence up. So, a smile slipped out. The look of relief on my husband's face was almost comical.

"Much, thank you, dear husband." I raised my eyebrows over my wine glass.

"And they say a way to a man's heart is through his stomach, ach! I think they got that wrong," Marcus murmured. "I think I'd rather face a hardened criminal then a ravenous wife."

"Best to remember that next time you decide to set fire to our dinner," I commented dryly, though there was a teasing look in my eye that he caught. Before I could react, he reached across the table and pulled me close to him.

"I'm not likely to forget," he grinned against my lips.

"See that you don't," I mumbled before kissing him.

As he went to reach for me again, I gave him a mischievous grin. "You're on clear-up." With that, I pulled away so his hands that had been happily exploring me were left touching thin air and scooped up our wine glasses. Walking towards our bedroom, I turned my head to look over my shoulder. Marcus still stayed in the same position, looking stunned.

"I'd hurry if I was you. Before I drink all the wine."

Smiling, I left him, leaving the bedroom door ajar.

In my contentment, the email was forgotten.

SOMETHING STIRRED HIM AWAKE.

Marcus turned to gaze out of the bedroom window. The moon was full, its aura luminescent, filling the room and covering them where they lay.

Sophia gave a soft moan in her sleep. He turned to her, moving to his side to stare down at her. She looked troubled, her face taut and anxious, when earlier in his arms it had been full of light.

What troubled her? He wished she would tell him, confide in him, instead of unnecessarily protecting him. *Was it the injury? Was it Richard? Or something more alarming?*

Reaching out, Marcus stroked back her hair in a soothing way, whispering to her in his Gaelic tongue *"Tha a h-uile càil gu math"*- all is well, as he had done many times over the last few weeks, until her face relaxed, and she grew still.

When he was sure Sophia slept peacefully once more, he lifted his hand from her face to gingerly touch her scar, starkly white in the moonlight, before slipping out of bed. Pulling on his jeans, he moved silently into the lounge and then to the front door, stepping out and closing it behind him.

Marcus grabbed a blanket from the outside seat and wrapped it around his shoulders against the chill of the night. He braced his hands on the wooden veranda.

The weight of the unsaid pressed down on him.

He had put in a request to visit Aneella where she was awaiting trial. It had been accepted but there had been a request from Aneella herself—she wanted to see Sophia. And that left him torn. As much as he felt she needed to see Aneella and finally confront her former friend, he was all too aware that Sophia was struggling with what had happened to her. She was without doubt suffering from PTSD, and this could set her back further. Which was the very last thing he wanted to happen.

But did he have the right to keep it from her?

Marcus sighed. He had been geared up to tell her while waiting for her to come home. Then a certain near fire, the threat of a hungry wife and a Sophia more relaxed-looking than she had looked for a long time gave him the excuse to reject it from his thoughts.

But now it weighed hard on him. He hated keeping secrets from her. And he hated that.

I CAME TO, realising I was alone in the bed. Rubbing my eyes, I peered at our bedside clock: 1:33am. Frowning, I climbed out of bed and padded my way across the bedroom, reaching for my robe. Making my way through the lounge and kitchen, not seeing Marcus, I headed to the only place I could think of him being: outside.

For a moment, I simply admired him, bathed in moon-light as he leaned on the wooden frame, a blanket around his shoulders. He looked so strong, an anchor against rough seas.

I moved behind him and felt him jolt with surprise as my arms came around his waist.

We were silent for a moment. Then I murmured, "Can't sleep?"

Marcus shook his head. "Something woke me up."

"And you chose to come out to into the freezing night air instead of staying cozy and warm with your wife?" I laughed.

He turned so we were facing each other. "Cold?"

"A little."

"Want to go back inside?"

I shook my head. "Not yet, the night is beautiful."

Marcus smiled. "Aye, that it is. Here, share my blanket."

With that, he opened the blanket and drew me against the warmth of his chest, encircling us both within the cocoon of the tartan. "Ahh, that's better. Shared body warmth has much to be praised. Especially in bonnie Scotland."

"Oh, I completely agree, Detective Inspector Armstrong. A much-underrated Scottish necessity."

I felt him chuckle and smiled.

We savoured the moment, relaxed in each other's arms as we gaze across at the moonlit loch, but I could sense something was on his mind.

"You know you should just tell me what's bothering you," I said quietly, turning to look at him. I tried to look relaxed, but inside my heart raced anxiously. Would he tell me what he'd been keeping back?

Marcus swivelled his head to stare down at me. A sweep of emotions crossed his face.

"I'm sure whatever it is, it won't scare me." My eyes searched to reassure him.

He nodded. "Perhaps not. But I'm afraid it will open memories you don't want to remember."

I waited, saying nothing. Marcus watched me closely, saw the determination in my eyes and give a strange half-sigh. "I've requested to see Aneella in prison."

The shock upon hearing her name made me jerk, despite my best efforts to try and appear nonchalant. He caught it—of course he caught it. His arms tightened around me.

"Why?" I managed to get out.

"I'm hoping she might feel more inclined to tell us more, now we know about... Richard. Perhaps she even will give us a clue as to how we can track him down. I know it's a long shot, but it's all I've got right now."

Richard. The sound of his name alone made me feel sick to the stomach. It's invaded me twice in one day. An over-whelming urge to tell him about the email swept over me. But I swallowed it down, leaving a bitter metallic taste in my throat. Soon, once I knew more, I would tell him, gladly.

Marcus was looking at me with concern. "Soph? You're worrying me, you look pale. Was I right to tell you?"

I took a deep breath and reached out to touch his cheek. "Yes, yes. You were. It's just a bit of a shock to hear their names. Let's hope the reality of her situation has sunk in and she'll be willing to talk."

"God, I hope so," he muttered, a dark look in his eyes. He closed his eyes for a moment, then in a rush, said, "She's asked if you will see her, in prison."

I stared at him. "What?"

Marcus reached out to cradle my face, his voice urgent. "You are under no obligation, none whatsoever. If you're not ready, if you need more time, we can go back and tell them. I don't care if it offends Aneella. You're the only one I care about. Or I can come with you. This is completely in your control, *mo leannan.*"

A hundred thoughts scattered in my head, none of them settling. "Can I have some time to think about it?"

Marcus reached down and gently kissed my forehead. "All the time in the world you need. You have nothing to fear, I won't let anything, or anyone harm you."

I pressed myself against him, holding him tightly, wanting so hard to believe him. But a strand of fear had entered my heart and somehow, I couldn't dislodge it, no matter how hard I clung to Marcus.

[4]

M arcus came up to his young sergeant, who seemed to be staring without looking at his computer.

"Everything all right there, Tom?"

Tom dragged his eyes away from the screen and, a little unfocused, stared up at Marcus. There was a moment of silence, Marcus watching intently, before Tom found his voice.

"Aye, aye ... just a text from a mate from my last station in Glasgow. He wants to see me..."

"That's good, though, right? If he's a mate and work colleague?" Marcus replied, trying to figure out why Tom seemed less than enthused by the idea of a meet up.

"Maybe. Anyway, what's on the job today, bos-sir?" Tom stood up, stuffing his phone into his pocket.

Marcus let him roll with it and motioned for Tom to follow him into his office. "Have a seat."

Tom did as requested and looked expectantly at Marcus. Marcus leaned against his desk and crossed his arms.

"I'm going to be visiting Ms. Blair at prison today.

You're up to date with the case notes for this one? I don't need to go over the details?"

Tom quickly shook his head earnestly. "No need at all. I'm completely up to date and grateful for your faith in me knowing this is a ... personal case for you."

Marcus gave a faint smile, appreciatively. "Aye. So, I think it would be good for you to come with me, listen in, give you some experience of what it's like talking to a suspect awaiting trial. Think you're up for that?'

Tom jumped up enthusiastically. "More than up for that! Thanks, boss!"

Marcus gave a small laugh, "'Sir,' Tom. It's 'sir.'"

"You know I'm never going to remember, right?"

A MILLION THOUGHTS were jousting for attention and none of them I truly wanted there. Thoughts about Aneella and whether I should visit her. What she would say to Marcus when he visited her today. Whether we would ever move past this. Then there were the guilty thoughts about keeping secrets from my husband. But the darkest thoughts were about Richard's email still haunting my inbox, and my thoughts.

I knew I had to reply. But the thought made my skin crawl.

"Come on, Sophia, time to fight back and stop being the victim." I muttered, letting out a breath as I leaned on the kitchen worktop nursing a coffee, staring at my laptop.

I moved over to the computer, sat down, and opened his email.

I'M SORRY. There, I've said it.

Now you're going to help me.

Don't let me down.

MY FINGERS BURNED, wanting to tell him exactly what I thought of him and where he could go. His audacity was unbelievable. I clenched my fist hard, trying to get my anger under control. Yet, at the same time I was rejoicing in this feeling that felt familiar yet wasn't. That spark I had lost after only just discovering it within me was pushing itself back out again, demanding to burst into flames.

Somehow this thought made me feel calmer, more in control. I was going to bring him out into the open, and together Marcus and I would take him down.

I hit reply and wrote:

WHAT DO you want from me?

AND, while my courage held, I pressed Send, then slowly sat back. Now, all I could do was pray I'd done the right thing.

Please God, protect us.

[5]

The thick impenetrable old walls around Her Majesty's Prison in Inverness loomed large and imposing before them.

It wasn't Marcus' first time visiting a prisoner awaiting trial, but every time he did, he felt the overwhelming urge to leave as soon as he was admitted to its deep chambers. It was almost as if the spirits of the entrapped still lingered in the stone. As they were escorted to the visitors waiting room, Marcus could feel Tom's eyes nervously darting everywhere.

"First time in here?" Marcus asked as calmly as he could, indicating for Tom to come and sit down beside him.

Tom nodded, gingerly taking the offered seat, noticeably quiet for him.

"It can feel quite imposing, ach? And that's exactly what it should feel like—a deterrent." Marcus grinned, injecting a bit of humour. "Stay on the right side of the law and you'll never need to enjoy its hospitality."

Tom gave a short laugh. "Aye, I intend to." He turned to Marcus; eyes bright. "I... uh... wanted to say thank you for taking me under your wing, so to speak. I appreciate it. I know I'm not the easiest of sergeants to manage. Or the most experienced, come to that."

A sudden, unexpected rush of protectiveness flowed through Marcus as he looked at his young sergeant. In so many ways, he saw the same eagerness in this young man to impress as Marcus himself had felt when he was a sergeant. He owed a lot to the first DI he'd worked for, Malcolm McAdam, who mentored and supported him even when he'd messed up. Which he did, a lot. Embarrassment washed over him. How Malcolm saw anything potential in him, he still didn't know. He was based in Glasgow now, retiring soon, but Marcus knew if he ever needed him, he would be there in a heartbeat.

"Experience will come over time, we all have to start somewhere, my friend. I was in your place once, hard as that is to believe. And, ach, you're not so hard to manage for a wee, uncouth lad," Marcus smiled.

Tom laughed, releasing some of the tension in his shoulders.

A shadow loomed over them. They looked up to see a prison officer staring down at them.

"Follow me."

Their footsteps echoed off the stark, grey walls as they followed the impossibly broad-shouldered officer to a smaller room away from the main visitor's hall. There was a table and three chairs, otherwise the room was bare, devoid of character as it had been designed to be.

Marcus and Tom sat down on the two chairs furthest away from the door. Without a word, the prison officer left them and closed the door.

Tom cast Marcus a perplexed look. "What happens now?"

"We wait for Ms. Blair to be escorted in. It won't be

long. They don't like to leave anyone unattended, not even the police."

Sure enough, within a couple of minutes, the door swung open. Aneella, escorted by a female officer, came into the room. As his gaze locked with hers, he had to fight to keep the shock from reaching his eyes. But inwardly, he shuddered. As she shuffled to the chair, sitting down slowly, as if in pain, Marcus saw the clothes were notice-ably hanging off her. Her skin was a pasty white and her blond hair hung lank and lifeless around her, where once it had been coiffed and styled within an inch of its life. Her once lively eyes were now dull and the skin around her eyes were dark as if bruised.

Frowning, Marcus turned to the officer standing by the door with her arms crossed.

"Is Ms. Blair being given sufficient amount of food?" he asked in quiet, yet authoritative voice.

The female officer bristled under his tone. "She's given the same portion as every inmate is. Whether she chooses to eat that or not is her responsibility, not ours. We don't force feed here... sir."

The last word was delivered with sarcasm, and Marcus had to fight not to react to it. Instead, clenching his jaw hard to swallow his thoughts, he turned to the shadow of a woman before him.

"Ms. Blair, this is DS Edgings." He cast a hand towards Tom, who gave a hesitant smile in her direction. "Thank you for seeing us today. Please let me know if there's anything you need, and I can see about getting it to you." He smiled as warmly as he could, hoping to put her at ease.

Aneella's eyes darted between them both. There was a small silence before she said, "What happened to the rottweiler who was your sergeant?"

Seeing a spark of her biting wit, just for the briefest

moment, gave Marcus hope that somewhere deep within her, she had not given up on life. His smile was genuine, his short laugh real as he answered, "DS Atkins and I came to a decision she was better off working in Glasgow."

"I'm sure your new sergeant here is much more malleable."

Tom shot Marcus a look, clearly unsure how to answer. Marcus came to his rescue. "He has his own particular set of skills."

"Where's Sophia? I told you I wanted to see her."

Marcus kept his calm composure, his gaze remaining on her. "She won't be coming today."

Aneella crossed her arms.

Marcus quickly asked, "Has your lawyer confirmed your date for your trial? I believe it's in six weeks."

She gave a small nod.

"Has he explained that you could be looking at a reduced sentence if you'd be willing to help us with this ongoing case? The judge will look more favourably on you when he passes the sentence. I'm sure you're keen to leave here as soon as you can."

She sat upright in her chair, an alertness in her eyes. "My lawyer is complete piece of crap. So, you tell me. What would I have to do?"

Marcus leaned forward, holding her in his steady gaze. "One thing. Just one thing ... you help us bring Richard in."

Aneella sat back, growing paler, if that was possible. She vehemently shook her head. "No ... no. I can't-"

"Ms. Blair, you need to start thinking about what's best for you," Marcus implored. "The longer you protect him, the worse this becomes for you." He took a breath. "Sophia nearly died at his hands. Do you want her blood staining your hands?'

She flushed and flashed him a hot, dark look. "That was beneath you, DI Armstrong. Don't try and guilt trip me."

At least I got a reaction. He gave a nod but didn't apologise. Instead, he changed tack and decided to try and appeal to her affection for Sophia, if she still carried any.

"Sophia needs closure," Marcus quietly said, his voice raw. "She can't move on until Richard is caught."

Aneella stared hard at him. "Are you sure it's her that needs closure … not you?"

Marcus could feel Tom's eyes boring into him, the prison officer's looming presence behind, and Aneella's daring challenge piercing him deeply. He could not, would not answer that—the truth was all too blatant to anyone paying attention.

"Will you help us, Ms. Blair?"

Silence. For the first time Tom piped up, "I would strongly recommend you do as DI Armstrong suggests."

"Do you now?" she said without even looking in Tom's direction, her focus still entirely on Marcus. He found himself involuntarily holding his breath. "Here's my deal. I will tell Sophia what I know. Only her. Make that happen and you have my co-operation."

As her words hit him hard in the gut, his immediate thought was *no way in hell.* He wouldn't put Sophia through that. He wouldn't let her be used in that way.

But as they stared at each other, he saw the faintest hint of desperation in her eyes, begging him to help her, and surprised himself by saying, "I will ask her." He fixed her with a hard look, his eyes narrowing. "But understand that I'm making no promises. And I won't let you hurt her again."

. . .

TOM MANAGED to restrain himself until they were out of the prison building and away from listening ears before it all burst out of him.

"Boss, why are we letting her dictate conditions to us?! She ought to be grateful we're helping her. I don't get it. Also, that place gave me the serious creeps." He gave a small shudder.

Marcus unlocked his car. He waited until they were both seated inside before replying. "Sometimes we have to play a game not of our own choosing, if it means we get the result we need. I don't like it any more than you do. I'll protect my wife above all else, make no mistake on that. But if Sophia agrees, we may be able to get Ms. Blair to open up. Right now, we are no further forward than we were three months ago, and we are fast running out of options."

"I get it, but it makes me feel a wee bit uncomfortable."

Marcus faintly smiled. "I'm glad it does. That means you have a good moral compass."

Tom, looking surprised, flushed a little. "I try to."

"Keep trying. Don't lose it."

Tom hesitated, as if wrestling with himself, then opened his mouth to reply. At that precise moment, his mobile phone rang loudly out through the air. Tom frowned then answered it. "DS Edgings... aye, he's here with me. We've just left Inverness Prison. Okay, we'll be there in five." Tom cut off the call and turned to Marcus who had been listening, alert and ready. "Looks like we have movement on the account. Jerry is watching it as we speak."

Before Tom had even finished speaking, Marcus was pulling away and accelerating down the road, blue lighting all the way.

. . .

THE COOL, sharp wind almost pushed me into the lodge as I let myself back in from my trip. I'd gone to Inverness after meeting for a coffee with an ex-client, Rachel, who'd quickly become a fast friend. I realised how much I needed this easy-going friendship. Rachel knew nothing about what happened to me, not because I didn't trust her, but that it was such a relief to be able to chat about everyday, nonsensical fun things. I hadn't had a friendship quite like that before, and it felt so good. Maybe one day, when all of this was finally over, I would tell her. But until then...

As I went to boil the kettle, rubbing my hands to warm them up, my mobile began to ring. I looked at the caller ID and smiled with delight.

"Cathy! It's so good to hear from you. How are you doing? Are you and Derek okay?"

There was the slightest pause before her voice came over the line. "Oh, we aren't too bad, my dear. As well as can be expected."

I settled myself into a chair, curling my legs under me. "Are you getting the extra help with Derek?"

Derek, her husband and Aneella's father, relied solely on Cathy to look after him. I hadn't seen them in a few months, though I had left a few messages. I worried about Cathy with the strain of looking after Derek and her only daughter awaiting trial.

I could hear the hesitation in her voice before she hastened to reassure me. "Oh yes, I'm getting help with bathing, which is much appreciated, that it is."

It didn't seem not nearly enough to me. "Well, it's a good start. Don't be afraid to ask for more. You're entitled to it and there's nurses trained to help with those recovering from a major stroke like Derek had. It would ease the strain on you."

"I will, my dear. But there's nothing anyone can really do for my Derek now."

My heart contracted. The thought of anything happening to Marcus was too awful to even imagine. To lose your husband slowly, painfully, day by day, week by week, was almost incomprehensible. "I'm so sorry," I whispered.

"You have nothing to be sorry about. If anything, it's me who should be asking for your forgiveness..."

As Cathy's voice trailed off, perhaps struggling to know how to continue, I felt icy fingers of dread grip my stomach —an urge to cut this conversation short before we went any further. But how could I? It wasn't Cathy's fault.

"No, really, you don't need to," I hastened to say. "Please don't worry."

"Oh Sophia, my dear, I must, though! What Ella has done... I never imagined my daughter capable of it. And then for you to be hurt, nearly die..." Her voice caught on the last word. There was a long silence as she fought to control her tears.

I squeezed my eyes shut, feeling the ice travel up my body as I fought hard to say the right thing. "I'm... all recovered. No permanent damage."

"I'm so relieved, I've been praying hard for that." There was another pregnant pause and I braced myself. "Sophia, my dear, I know I have no right to ask this. But one day when you are a mother yourself, you'll realise you can never stop loving them no matter what. You can never stop protecting them. Ella won't let me see her, no matter how many times I beg her to send me a visitor's pass. I'm so worried. I—don't know who else to ask." The next words came out in a rush. "Would you go and visit her for me?"

Even though I sensed the words coming, they shook me to my core. I breathed out slowly. *How could I ever want to see your daughter again?* came my immediate, perhaps selfish response. What could I possibly say to help in any way?

"I'm not sure she would want to see me," I lied. Marcus had said so only this morning.

"Oh, but she does! She told me herself, my dear. I truly think she wants to ask for your forgiveness." *If only.* "I know I'm asking so much from you, far more than I should. But please, will you at least consider it?"

Oh dear God... I had to turn away and clear the sudden tightness in my throat, before reluctantly saying, "Yes, okay. But, Cathy, I can't make you any promises."

"Oh, thank you, thank you so much. You have such a good heart, my dear."

As we hung up a few moments later, I felt myself being pulled towards something I couldn't control or stop. And I had no idea what the hell to do.

[6]

"Tell me what we've got, Jerry."

Marcus, with Tom skidding to a halt behind him, leaned over Jerry's shoulder to stare at the screen.

Jerry replied without looking up. "I noticed a new account that follows the same pattern as the others has opened up, with a similar data code system. I'm expecting any minute now we will see money begin to move into it, if its following the usual pattern."

Marcus turned to Tom. "I need the location where they are transmitting from."

"On it, boss." Tom picked up his phone and leapt over to his computer.

As if by magic, the account erupted to life, with a pound at a time dropping in rapid succession. Marcus felt the adrenaline rush through him as he started the stopwatch on his watch.

"We've got exactly three minutes before this will cut off."

"Jerry, get as much intel as you can, especially on the codes." Jerry nodded.

"Stay focused, team," Marcus continued. "We need to act fast to get enough evidence. We can't lose this one."

He looked at his watch. Fifty-five seconds had passed. Marcus scanned the numbers flashing past, trying to find a pattern. The account balance had already surpassed £300,000.

"Two minutes left. What've you got for me, Jerry?"

"Give me a minute," Jerry muttered.

'We don't have much more! What about you, Tom?"

Tom, speaking rapidly into the phone, held up his hand.

Two minutes and five seconds passed.

"Less than a minute left before we lose transmission," Marcus warned, videoing the screen to help him scan for clues later. There were definitely similarities here that matched previous fraudulent accounts—which meant they were either getting sloppy or confident. Either way, Marcus felt a sweet, sharp triumph that he may finally have had something tangible to work with.

Twenty seconds remaining.

"I'm nearly there with the location."

Marcus walked over to Tom, watching the map system home in on the outskirts of Glasgow.

"Good. See if you can pinpoint a house, street, anything. We've got ten seconds. Don't stop!"

Ten seconds wasn't nearly enough.

Jerry's screen flashed: TRANSMISSION LOST. The screen went decidedly blank.

"Dammit," Marcus muttered. He took a deep breath, forcing down the frustration he always felt when faced with this ridiculously short window timed to ensure the corrupt fraud ring could never be shut down. "Give me some good news, someone. Anyone."

Jerry and Tom looked at each other, then Marcus.

"The codes are definitely following the same number system," Jerry offered.

Marcus nodded vigorously, coming closer to Jerry. "Good. Really good. This means they are getting too lazy. We can jump on this to catch them. Give me all the data and evidence you've got and put it on my desk. That's all I want you working on right now, aye?"

"Aye," Jerry nodded, turning back to his computer.

Marcus turned to Tom. "How did we get on with that location fix in Glasgow?"

Tom was looking at him gravely and Marcus, disappointment coursing through him, reminded himself that his sergeant was still young and learning.

Then Tom grinned, "I've got you an address, Boss!"

Marcus' eyes widened, then he gave a loud whoop that had the whole bay looking up. "You wee beauty!"

"Does this mean I can carry on calling you 'Boss?'"

"You can call me anything you like if you keep getting me these kinds of results," Marcus grinned, gripping Tom on the shoulder.

A beam lit up the young man's face.

THE COLD, insipid walls were even more oppressive today. Aneella squeezed her eyes shut and tried to pretend she was anywhere but in this small cell, pressed against the door.

For a tantalising moment, she could almost feel the warmth of the sun caressing her skin, the sound of the waves crashing against the rocks, the dazzling light of the ochre blue sky. A hand as it teased its way down her body, causing a shiver of pleasure down her spine—

"Are you gonna bloody move or not? I want my wee grub even if you don't."

The harsh, annoyed voice of her cellmate brought her sharply back to the present. Reluctantly opening her eyes, she met the glare of Stella, who could be any age from 40 to 65 with that sour look, broad shoulders, and unkempt hair. Aneella's lawyer had tried to get her in a cell, even though that wasn't common practice while awaiting trail. But it appeared the justice system wasn't falling for that trick and had decided to put her with a convicted prisoner, already on her third time in prison for felony and grievous bodily harm. Perhaps because they were pissed off they were asked. Maybe they thought it would shake her up enough to spill everything about Richard and those they had worked for. Only in her weakest moment would she ever fall for that. Until then, she wouldn't give them that satisfaction. Not once.

MY HEART LIFTED upon seeing his name on my phone. Smiling, I answered on the second ring, walking into the lounge. "Well, a call during daylight hours. To what do I owe such an unexpected honour?"

I heard his deep chuckle. "Can a husband not call his wife, ach, with no other motive but to hear her dulcet English tones?"

"Can a husband tell when his wife is looking skeptical at him over the phone?"

"Mmm, I think he can possibly deduce that."

I grinned, forgetting the emotions my phone call with Cathy had stirred, calming down as I always did when I heard his voice. Sometimes I caught the most tantalising glimpse of it always being like this when we no longer had Richard and Aneella pressing down on us. And it brought such a rush of joy, I could have wept with it. "Glad to see your detective skills are being put to use for something."

"Aye, tease me now, English lass, but be warned I may need to show you my very thorough detective skills later."

"Oh, I really hope you do," I teased, curling up on the sofa.

I could hear Marcus quietly laughing, then what sounded like his door shutting. "As much as I would love to continue this very enjoyable conversation—"

"I'm sure you would."

He ignored my cheeky quip. "I need you to come to me here at the station."

That took me aback. Since we'd been married, I hadn't been near the station, nor had I wanted to be. So why now? Then it hit me hard, and my teasing tone turned strained. "Is this because of Aneella?"

A small pause. "Aye, aye it is."

I let out a breath. "Can we not talk later at home?"

I could hear his measured breathing as he sought to find the right words to convince me. I squeezed my eyes shut as he said, "Ach, I don't want to bring this into our home, the one place that's just about you and me. So would you come here?" And when I didn't answer immediately, "Trust me, *mo leannan*, I wouldn't ask this of you unless it was of utmost importance."

I did trust him, more than anyone else in this world. "Okay," I said. "I'll be there in an hour."

IT WAS with mixed trepidation I found myself standing outside the modern doors of Inverness Police station. My mind flew back to that first time I'd stood outside, reluctant to walk in and face Marcus, determined to believe the best of Ella. How wrong I'd gotten that—trusting those who didn't deserve it and doubting the one person who would save me in every way possible.

Pushing the door open, I walked up to the duty police officer at the front desk, smiling warmly at her. She smiled back, looking taken aback.

"May I help you?"

"Hi, I'm Sophia, DI Armstrong's wife. He's expecting me."

Her eyes widened, "Oh, of course. I'll let him know you're here. Do you know the way?"

I nodded, smiled again. "I do, thank you."

Sure enough, within a few minutes, despite a confusing mass of corridors, I found myself walking through the open area leading to Marcus' office, his door agape. As I looked to where he sat at his desk, a warm feeling flowed through me. It was here, in that office, that I'd first dared to push our relationship from detective and suspect to lovers. I wasn't sure where I'd mustered the courage, but Marcus somehow always awoke something in me that drew me to him with a new boldness.

Marcus sensed my presence and looked up, beckoning me over with that faint smile of his, coming to the door to greet me.

"On time as ever," he praised as he kissed me on the cheek.

"I try," I murmured, feeling eyes upon us, turning my head a little to see two men watching us, one young and grinning, and one older and more reserved in appearance. "Friends of yours?" I commented, sliding my eyes in their direction.

Marcus half-smiled at them. "Aye. Remember I told you

about my new sergeant, Tom? I want you to meet him. He's a good lad."

I raised my eyebrows as I said, "I think I would like anyone who was your sergeant after Morven."

Marcus chuckled as he guided me over to them, mumbling, "Let's try to forget that name, shall we?" Then, in a louder voice, "Tom, Jerry, I'd like you to meet my wife, Sophia."

Refraining the urge to comment on the whole Tom and Jerry thing going on, which took quite a bit of willpower, I smiled warmly at them both. "It's lovely to meet you both."

"Likewise." Jerry nodded, giving me a shy smile.

Tom stood and held his hand out to me. Amused, I put mine in his, and he brought it to his mouth and kissed it. I turned in surprise to my husband, who was giving his sergeant a rather narrow-eyed look.

"Have to say the wee boss man has got himself a good-looking wife." He turned to Marcus with a cheeky grin. "Not sure how you managed that—"

"Aye, and you can stop right there," Marcus said pointedly. "In fact, I would heartily recommend you do."

I bit my lip to stop myself from laughing as I extracted my hand from young Tom, who was looking a bit sheepish. "Right, sorry boss- sir. But she is gorgeous."

"No arguments from me there, sergeant. I have fine taste."

I did laugh then, giving Tom a warm smile. "Thank you, Tom. As I'm probably old enough to be your mum, I will happily accept that compliment."

Tom's grin almost broke his face. Marcus stepped in and steered me off rather efficiently. "Wait till you're out of breeches before you try and chat my wife up. Back to work."

Tom did as instructed.

"Aww, I rather like your new sergeant," I teased as we walked into his office. "He has exceptional taste."

Marcus gave me a look of warning. "Don't encourage him. He's a mere wee whelp, and you would eat him alive."

"Would I now?"

"Aye, and you know it." Shutting the door after us, he steered us towards the back corner of his office where we couldn't be seen and pulled me towards him. "You're enjoying this a little too much, Mrs. Armstrong. Getting me back for Morven, are you?"

I placed my hands on his chest. "As if I would make such a calculated, low move," I murmured, letting my hands move down a little, enjoying the darkening of desire in Marcus' eyes. "You know, there was one thing I wanted you to do in this office that you never did."

His hands touched the skin exposed between my shirt and jeans, sending a tingling jolt through me. "And that was?"

I leaned closer still. "Kiss me... to start with, at least."

"Now that wouldn't have been very professional," he said, even as his lips moved across my jawline before moving down my neck and throat. I sighed softly and brought my hands up to his neck to hold him there. "Seeing as you were a suspect." His words reverberated against my skin.

"Since when have we let that stop us?" I managed to get out, before dragging his head up to meet my eager lips. He didn't need any persuasion, pulling us into a deep kiss as he pressed me back against the wall, knocking over files onto the floor. His hands were under my shirt and probably would have disposed of it too, if not for the ringing of his phone cutting through the heat between us.

Cursing under his breath, Marcus reluctantly let me go and reached for the phone, answering it with a curt, "Aye?"

A little flushed, and more than a little frustrated, I attempted to smooth down my shirt and hair and began picking up the files scattered on the floor. As my eyes moved over one of the files, the blood began to rush to my head ... until the letters spelling out my name on top of the case file began to swim before me. I blindly reached out and grabbed the desk to steady myself. A shooting pain in my side where the knife had plunged in had me forcing back bile. My stomach lurched. Beads of sweat broke out on my forehead.

"Listen, I need to call you back." The phone went down, sound of footsteps moving around to where I was still crouched, unable to move. I felt the warm touch of his hand as it covered mine still clutching the file, and his other on my elbow, carefully drawing me up till I was level with him. He raised my chin until I had no choice but to look at him. I couldn't seem to find any words to say or stop my hand shaking. He gave a sigh, then bent his forehead forward until it rested on my brow.

"I'm sorry." His voice was just above a whisper. "I should have warned you that you would see your file. I didn't consider the effect it would have on you."

"It's okay." I managed to say, hating the tremor in it. "Of course, you would have a file on me. Of course, you would. I—I think it was just the shock of seeing it ... seeing my name like that and—and it becoming a reality. That sounds ridiculous, I know it happened..."

Marcus was drawing back, shaking his head, framing my face as he said with a note of urgency, "No, it's not ridiculous. You never imagined this would happen to you, that this is our reality. But we'll find a way to finish this and give you closure, I promise."

His eyes held a fierce determination that convinced me more than his words did.

"I know we will."

Marcus gently extracted the file from my hand and put it down on his desk. Then he pulled me into his arms, and I gratefully sank into the shelter that his body gave me. We stayed locked together until he sensed I was steadier, then he stepped back and guided me over to the chairs I had sat on the first time I'd come in here. Which felt like a million years ago.

"You're not about to question me, are you?" I gave a small smile, trying to lighten the mood with my poor attempt of a joke.

Marcus returned the smile. "Should I?"

My eyes narrowed, "I'm wise to that cunning method of yours of answering a question with a question, Detective Armstrong."

"Is that so?"

"Mmm, keep that for some other unsuspecting poor soul," I answered dryly.

He laughed, then his features took on a more serious look. "Soph..." he began, then paused, as if unsure how to proceed, which was unusual for my husband.

I decided to make it easier for him, leaning forward to lay my hand over his. "Just tell me. I won't break."

I felt his fingers curl around mine, clasping them tight. His eyes locked with mine. "You know I went to visit Aneella today to see if she would be more willing to tell me where Richard is, or who he is working for?" After I nodded, he continued, "She... isn't in a great place, mentally or physically."

"Should I feel sorry for her?" I blurted, feeling the heat of anger rush through me.

Marcus kept his eyes steady on me, continuing in that mild manner of his that at times, like now, drove me mad with frustration. "I'm not telling you this to force you to feel pity or guilt towards her. I'm painting a realistic picture of the situation before I ask you to do something that will carry a cost."

My heart began to beat erratically. Marcus took my silence as permission to continue. "Despite my best efforts, she refused to reveal anything more to me. But she made one offer—she will tell everything she knows to you... only you."

I stared at him, swallowing hard. "Me?" My stomach clenched.

"Aye." He reached out and cradled my flushed cheek. "I won't force you into this, it needs to be your choice alone."

"But if I don't, she won't say anything, and we'll know nothing more?"

I watched Marcus' face carefully and saw confirmation in his eyes even as he said, "There are always other ways."

"Her mum, Cathy, called me today," I said. Marcus frowned at my words, looking taken aback. "She was practically begging me to go and see Aneella. She's so worried about her, especially as Aneella won't let her visit." I looked down for a moment, composing myself, drawing on the inner resolve that lingered there, despite the fear that I'd lost it forever. "It's hard enough to say no to her, with the desperation I heard in her voice. But to say no to the man I love, to my husband when I know you would have tried everything before asking this... So yes, I'll go and see her." I covered his hand with mine, which still cradled my cheek. "For you. And for Cathy."

An array of emotions washed over Marcus' eyes as he looked intently at me. "You are incredible," he uttered, "braver than anyone I know."

I gave him a faint smile, fighting back tears. "I am when I'm with you. Your love makes me strong."

My last word was lost on his mouth as he pulled me

into an urgent kiss before crushing me to him. As I circled my arms around his neck, I found myself praying for the strength I would need to face Aneella—and that my secret of making contact with Richard wouldn't ultimately destroy us.

[7]

The day was drawing to dusk when Tom walked out of the police station, popping his jacket collar against the brisk wind. Winter was eagerly biting away at autumn, and it wouldn't be long before it won the fight.

The adrenaline rush of the day had ebbed away a while ago, and Tom found a tiredness entering his bones. He was meant to be meeting a mate for a drink, but right then, all he felt like doing was heading back to his flat and praying like mad that his flatmate, Alex, was out. Alex was a good laugh, but sometimes he was too much.

Tom was rounding a street corner away from the head-quarters when a figure stepped out from behind a tree. He instinctively stepped back, his senses kicking into alert.

"Tom?"

Hearing the woman's soft, distinctive voice, Tom relaxed. A different kind of energy buzzed through him as she stepped closer, the last of the rays illuminating her face. Her hazel eyes looked drawn and clouded with anxiety.

"Libby? Ach, you gave me a scare. What are you doing here?"

"Looking for you." She chewed on her lip. "You didn't reply to my text earlier."

Tom clapped his forehead. "I clean forgot! I'm sorry, it's been a crazy kind of day."

Libby nodded, turned her head away. She looked a little shivery in her thin, cropped top that did nothing to protect her from the cold. Tom resisted the desire to give her his coat even though he wanted to. Badly.

"Tell me now what you said," he urged, stepping closer.

Libby looked around her, her eyes darting in both directions. "Can we go somewhere more private?"

That was when he felt an ominous feeling clench in the pit of his stomach.

"Aye. We can go to mine... if Jake won't mind."

Her eyes flew up to his. "Jake doesn't need to know."

His stomach twisted. This would only lead to trouble. But feeling like the fool that he was, Tom nodded and led her along to his flat not far away. He silently prayed that Alex was out. With trepidation, he turned the key in the lock, and called out as he swung the door open.

"Alex, mate, you there?"

No reply. Tom breathed out in relief, then turned to give Libby a smile that appeared more confident than he felt, something he had mastered over the last years.

They walked into his humble kitchen. Libby was looking around with interest and he briefly wondered what she was thinking. It was the first time they had ever been alone—usually her boyfriend was stuck to her side. Tom bitterly regretted the day he introduced his so-called mate, Jake, to the girl he was crazy about. His mate had then done the worst kind of betrayal by charming Libby into going out with him, leaving Tom watching from the sidelines. It was his own damn fault for never telling Libby how he felt about her despite meeting at college six years ago and had hung around in the same circle of friends ever since.

"Uh, can I get you anything?" he found himself saying, feeling like a right numpty.

She turned and smiled at him, the first smile she had given him in too long a time. It knocked the breath out of him, and he found himself grinning stupidly back.

"No, no, I'm good, thanks."

"Do you want to sit down?" Tom waved towards the old, somewhat messy sofa filled mostly with rubbish and old magazines his flatmate never bothered clearing up. When she shook her head, he muttered, "Aye, don't blame you. I don't like sitting on it most days."

Libby smiled again, though this time with more strain, then walked over to the mantel shelf over the rusty, black soot-ridden fireplace that their landlord was supposed to be clearing out. She started fiddling with scrap pieces of paper and abandoned keys.

Tom stared at her tense back, unsure of what to do next. He couldn't help asking himself, *what would the boss do?* Marcus had more patience than humanly possible, and Tom knew he would wait it out until Libby finally confessed to whatever was weighing her down.

He wasn't Marcus.

No way was he waiting, not when a flatmate could walk in on them at any minute.

"Want to tell me what's happened? You've never come to me like this before, so I know it's got to be pretty major."

Instead of answering him, Libby stilled, her back to him. Frustration and a sense of urgency gripped Tom. "Listen, if you're worried about telling me—"

Suddenly, she was in his arms, crushing him so hard he felt the breath rush out of him like he'd been pierced. Initial shock turned to all over warmth as he found himself pressed against her, his arms coming around her far too easily. He had never held her close before. She'd never been one for physical touch: always a protective wall around her. This should have sounded off more alarm bells in his mind. But right then, he was finding it hard to concentrate on anything except how unbelievably good it felt having her body against his.

"I'm in trouble." Libby's words, wobbly and a little tearful, were mumbled against his shoulder, and he had to strain to catch them. "I mean deep-shit-filled trouble, the kind that gets me into jail. I'm scared—I don't know what to do."

She's not the only one. Tom forced himself to take a step back and hold her at arm's length so he could see her face. Her mascara had run with her tears, which he gently wiped away as if it was the most natural thing in the world to do.

"You need to start by telling me about this trouble that you think could land you in jail."

Libby looked down, then reluctantly raised her eyes to meet his. "I ... took some drugs to a buyer from the dealer."

Tom swore, feeling a sweat break out on his forehead as her words hit home. Libby rushed on, as he grappled with the reality of what she'd confessed to. "It's only been the once, I've never done it before—you've gotta believe me! But I think I was spotted by an undercover police officer."

He swore again, letting go of her and taking some steps back. He could feel her anxious eyes on him. Right then, he felt every inch the inexperienced twenty-four-year-old he was. Tom dragged his slightly shaking fingers through his hair and tried to think. Something about Libby doing this was completely out of character. She had never touched drugs or anything like that, had always worked hard at school. Someone must have persuaded her to do it, apply pressure on her, someone she was devoted to...

"Tell me truthfully, and don't lie." Tom stopped pacing and came up close to her. He took a deep breath. "Is Jake the dealer?"

If he hadn't been watching her with intensity, he would have missed the flicker of recognition that he had guessed accurately before it was smothered out, and she was the one turning away from him. "Does it matter who the dealer is?"

"Of course it matters!" His reply came out more explosively than he intended, but too late to rein it in. "You're not the kind of girl to do this shit stupid stuff ... unless it was for someone you loved." He spun her around, forcing her to face him. "And there's only one person who that fits for. Why, damn it, *why*?"

Libby's eyes began to fill with tears. "I didn't know how to say no to him! He told me that if I loved him, I would do this for him—I know, shit, I know how that sounds, how dumb I was. I—" She grabbed his t-shirt in her hands, beseeching him. "Tom, please, do one thing for me, just one thing and I swear I won't ask for anything more."

He felt the axles of his world begin to spin as he stared into her deep brown eyes. She looked at him as if he was the only one who could save her. He knew what was coming, knew before she uttered one word that he wouldn't be able to refuse her. Not when she clutched him like this, or pleaded to him with her tears. He hadn't never known he was this weak until now.

"All you need to do is see if there's been a police report filed on me. I'm sure you've got access to records or something. That's it, that's all I'm asking for."

Except they both knew it wouldn't be all, that she would ask him for more, and more, and more.

"I could get struck off the force for this, you realise that?"

"Please. I'm dying here. You've got to help me."

A REPLY WAS SITTING in my inbox when I logged back on. Author unknown.

Who are you trying to fool?

A pulse in my neck quickened. My palms felt sweaty. Slowly, carefully, as if it was about to explode in my face, I opened the email.

WHEN YOU GOING to stop messing with me
and give me a time and place to meet.
This isn't a game, Soph.
Don't make me turn nasty.

[8]

M arcus noticed I was quieter than normal that
evening, but he must have put it down to us going
to visit Aneella in the morning. I wanted to believe it
myself. Somehow it seemed so much better than Richard's
deliberately manipulative words that had constricted my
chest. I needed to work out where I could safely meet him,
and then how the hell I could get him to tell me who he
was working for and where he was staying. Then, and only
then, when I had something concrete, would I tell Marcus
so he could arrest Richard. In the meantime, I *had* to stay
strong and focused.

That night, when the hour had grown still, I began to
dream again. I was climbing a mountain, one that seemed
oddly familiar. My feet ached as my heart pounded nine-
teen to the dozen with the strain of the pace I set. Sweat
was running uncomfortably down my spine, and the air felt
thinner the higher I climbed. The wind whipped my hair
and stung my eyes. I kept climbing, something driving me
on, as if I couldn't stop. Every time I thought I had reached
the summit, there would be another peak towering higher

into the sky, majestic and impenetrable. Then, I would again climb and climb, never stopping until, finally, I reached the last summit. Yet just as I did, the rocks beneath me began to shake, knocking me off my feet. I scrambled to grab on to something, anything, to stop myself from falling. Panic built up again as my body started to slip over the edge—

I awoke with a violent jolt, shaking with adrenaline. I looked over at my sleeping husband, and somehow his calmness brought me rapid comfort. Settling back down, I curled up against his solid warmth, trying to disperse the shuddering, lingering feeling of falling.

It was a long time before I fell back asleep.

MARCUS WATCHED his wife carefully as they both went through their normal morning routine. She stood in the shower, almost immobile as the hot water cascaded over her, the silhouette of her naked body so tantalising he was fighting the urge to go and press himself against her until he helped her forget everything except the two of them.

All at once, his mind flashed back to walking in and finding her weeping on the floor, his towel clutched to her, after he had pulled her out of the loch and brought her back to here. That was the first time he'd nearly lost her and realised he was falling in love, that her life was all that mattered. His gut twisted as he remembered the blind fear of trying to find her under the murky water. He swallowed hard. Dammit, they deserved to be free of this once and for all. Sophia deserved happiness, and he would give her that, no matter what it cost him.

Before he was even aware he was doing it, Marcus was stripping off his clothes as he walked into the bathroom, stepping into the shower and pulling a startled Sophia against him. His mouth was on hers almost desperately as he pressed her back against the tiles, cradling her face in his hands, feeling her respond to him as skin met skin.

"Marcus?" She managed to get out breathlessly when his mouth dragged itself off hers and began to trail kisses down her neck. His hands roamed over her breasts, then down to her hips, to pull her tight against himself. She clutched his shoulders, her leg moving instinctively around his hip so his hand could grip it and caress her skin.

He lifted his head to meet her gaze as the water drenched them. "Let me love you," he murmured. "Let me kiss you, fill you, bring you pleasure." He watched her eyes fill with lust, then she met him with a hungry kiss that made his breath catch. Within moments he was deep inside her, setting a rhythm that had them both gasping with urgency as the pace became more frantic... and then came the sweet release they both desperately craved.

THE SKY WAS heavy with storm clouds as we drove the relatively short distance to HMP Inverness Prison. I was trying to remain upbeat and hide my nerves, not that I thought for one minute I had convinced Marcus with my poor acting skills. That man knew me more intimately than anyone ever had. But I wanted to go in strong, for myself, not just for him. So, I chatted incessantly all the way about complete, utter crap and Marcus smiled and nodded like I was imparting pearls of wisdom as he concentrated on the road ahead. I don't think I had ever loved him more.

We arrived at the last place I wanted to be. As I stared up at the imposing dark walls, my throat constricted, and my words vanished. I tried to swallow, but it only seemed to make the hard lump in my throat worse.

We drove up to the security gate and stopped. Marcus

lowered his window and showed the security man his police ID and gave my name. The man glanced over at me, looked at his clipboard with the visitor's list and nodded. The gate opened. Marcus drove through and parked in one of the allocated visitor spots. He turned the engine off then turned to me. He reached across and wrapped his large, warm hand around my cold one.

"Ready?"

No! my body silently screamed. Instead, I gave the barest nod. Marcus gave me a reassuring smile then opened his door, giving me no choice but to do the same.

As we emerged into the cold air, Marcus took my hand again and I gave him a grateful smile.

"It's this way."

I followed him through the main entrance doors. The minute my foot hit the concrete floor, I had the overwhelming urge to bolt. The feeling of being enclosed and trapped within was immediate. I bit down hard on my lip.

We were shown through a confusing blur of corridors and more security checks by bored guards before finally coming to a room filled with a few rows of tired-looking plastic seats. The guard told us to wait there. I perched on one of the uncomfortable chairs, vaguely aware of Marcus sitting down beside me.

My eyes travelled around the soulless waiting room, wondering who else had sat in this very seat, every nerve in their body tight and painful as they prepared to face whoever they came to see. Perhaps it was someone they loved, and they couldn't comprehend what happened to have their loved one end up here.

What was I going to say to her? What could she want to tell me?

I became aware that my name was being said. My eyes finally focused on Marcus, who was leaning close to me.

"Are you alright, *mo leannan?*" His voice was low, slightly urgent. "You can change your mind about seeing Aneella anytime, you know that? You would be no less brave if you chose not to see her."

Don't give me a way out of this. It would be too easy to nod, and let Marcus take me out of here.

But there was a deeper part of me that couldn't allow myself to become that woman I had been under Aneella's control, with no self-confidence or belief in herself. I was finally beginning to acknowledge I no longer wanted to be her victim.

Straightening my shoulders, I looked my husband fully in the eyes. "No, I can do this."

There was a spark of love in his nod, and immediately I felt calmer.

"Here, wear this."

Surprised, I felt his fingers unzip my coat and attach a microphone.

Marcus quietly said. "I don't believe for one minute she'll talk while I'm in the room with you. But I need to know exactly what she says. This is the best way. I'll be listening throughout."

Before I had time to reply, the guard was back.

"Ms. Blair is ready to see you."

I briefly closed my eyes, breathing out. Too much rested on this and I couldn't mess it up.

It was time to face someone who had once been my friend, and now was my adversary.

[9]

I stared at Aneella, unable to hide the pity I felt. My God, how had she altered so much in such a short time?

Sensing that neither of us knew what to say in that moment, Marcus encouraged me to sit down in the only other chair in the room. That jerked Aneella into action. She glared hard at Marcus, showing a burning ember of annoyance that he was in the room. It was such an Ella thing to do, it strangely put me at ease.

"You said I could talk alone with Sophia."

Marcus raised an eyebrow at Aneella. "And I keep my promises." He turned to me, asking me with his eyes if I was ready. I gave a nod and he returned it with the faintest smile on his face. Then he turned back to Aneella and said with a steely tone, "I'll be right outside, and the door will remain open at all times."

She had the sense not to argue with him. We both felt him leave. I couldn't look away from Aneella. There was a long silence that we both seemed unsure of how to break. My mind whirled with all the things to confront her about... and absolutely no idea how to bring them out. I also needed to keep focused on why I was here. If doing it Marcus' way meant that we got the information we needed without me having to meet Richard, then I had to stay sharp and do everything in my power to get her to open up. It was worth sacrificing my pride for that.

Trying not to self-consciously touch the hidden microphone under my coat collar, I broke the silence with a soft question. "Are you okay?"

She was thrown off. Her forehead creased as she stared at me.

"You've lost weight." I added, perhaps unnecessarily. "Are you eating?"

Aneella's glance flickered to the officer with an ironic smile. "It's not exactly Michelin-star food here." She gave a snort, which the officer studiously ignored. I found myself smiling faintly.

"You need to eat."

"Why?" She shot back at me. "Does it matter what happens to me? Do you care?"

Do I? I'd spent so long trying not to think about her, hurt by her betrayal, I had pushed down my former love for her, my willingness to do anything to help her. I settled for, "I don't want to see you mistreat yourself."

"Even now, you can't help but try to see something worth saving in me. I told you, some people are rotten through and through." Her words carried bitterness, and her eyes were dull.

There was a slump in her posture that told me she was weakening. I had to pounce on that now, even if it made me feel like a heel. I leaned forward.

"Ella," my affectionate name for her slipping out without me even realising, "you have to start helping yourself here. You can't let them leave you to take the rap for this crime. Talk to me, tell me who you were working for, and for the love of all things, stop protecting Richard. He doesn't deserve anyone's loyalty."

At the sound of his name, Aneella's head snapped up. Now she leaned forward, fixing me with a hot intensity that made me want to move instinctively back. "Have you heard from Richard?"

My heart lurched. *She couldn't possibly know!*

ANYONE ELSE WOULD HAVE MISSED the widening of Sophia's pupils, the little indrawing of breath, and the quick glance towards the door as if she was afraid her DI would hear.

But not her. Oh no, not her. She knew Sophia, she *knew* her former friend.

White-hot anger surged through her at the thought that he had the audacity to contact his former wife after swearing blindly that he would play this her way.

"No, no of course not."

You lie!

"Ella?"

Her voice held a note of caution, trepidation. Wise girl.

But who should fear her the most right then?

As I said her name, my nerves screamed and my brain furiously tried to get my body back in control. I forced myself to meet her hot gaze.

"Something you wanted to tell me, Sophia?" came her too calm reply, and by doing so sparking a similar anger in me.

"There's lots I want to tell you, to make you understand what I've gone through in the last few months! But would it do any good, huh? Would you feel the least bit remorseful?" I pushed. "I won't play your games anymore, Aneella."

There was a long, tense silence. She studied me as if I had morphed into someone she didn't recognise.

"You have five minutes left." The bland voice of the officer cut into the air.

I stared her down, feeling stronger than I had in a long time. "Start talking."

And then I waited, holding my breath.

Sophia hadn't given way in defeat as she would have once done, cunningly turning the tables back round. For the first time, Aneella felt a grudging respect for this woman sitting before her.

Maybe it was because of this, maybe because of a sudden unadulterated fear that everything was slipping out of her control, but something gave way in her in that startling moment, a small crack loosening her carefully constructed walls.

It was time they started moving to her demands, like the puppets on the string that they were.

. . .

IT WAS like I could see the inner battle raging within her. The insistent ticking of the clock was beginning to wreak havoc on my nerves, every second a chance lost to persuade her to talk. Yet I held back, determined to make her be the first to break the stand-off.

"Do you remember what I use to call Richard back in our uni days? Apart from Bastard, that is."

I stared at her. "Ella, stop playing games."

It was like I hadn't spoken. Her finger began moving in circles on the table in almost a hypnotic way and I found myself drawn to the motion.

"Come on, you can't have forgotten. Don't play dumb. We were in that student bar—you know, the one we always went to. And you were sulking because Rich was being his usual arrogant self and went off chatting to some girls." Although she wasn't looking up at me, I could feel the intensity of words. "What did I call him? Think hard, Soph."

I was grappling here, like a blind person lost in a crowd. Was she playing her usual mind games or trying to tell me something significant? My eyes followed her finger, which seemed to be moving in the form of a letter, like the letter—

There was a loud, exasperated exclamation from Aneella. "You're not thinking hard enough!"

"Okay, time's up." The prison officer stepped forward as if to take Aneella right there and then. From outside, Marcus moved to the doorway.

"No, wait!" I practically shouted, reaching out towards Aneella as if I could physically stop her from being taken away. "Please, for what we once were to each other, help us find him," I implored her.

Her eyes burned into me, even as we both stood up and the officer came up alongside her. "I am, can't you see that?" she muttered. Her finger traced the same letter on my hand resting on the table. Frowning, I stared down, watching her movement as if hypnotised.

I inhaled sharply.

It was the letter S.

[10]

Tom glanced surreptitiously around him, nervous sweat oozing out of him. He hated this, going behind his boss's back. She had him right where she wanted him.

The police station was unusually quiet, and thus, ideal. Marcus was at Inverness HMP Prison with his wife, Jerry and Dan were chasing on a lead, and no one else was taking much notice of him. It had to be now.

Sitting down at the end computer that was the best concealed from passers-by, Tom quickly logged in and went to the search database used to access records and arrests. His heart felt like it was about to explode out of his chest. Technically, no one accessed records unless they were relevant to their case and this could lead a trail back to him—but he would just have to wing it if that happened. He drummed his fingers impatiently on the desk as he waited for it to load. When it finally did, he crouched over the keyboard, typed in *'Elizabeth Archer'*, then held his breath.

'NO RECORDS FOUND', the computer blinked at him.

His relief was palpable and immediate. Tom gave an internal whoop of delight. *Thank God.*

Grinning, he went to quickly log out, when he felt a shiver of apprehension course through him. Acting on instinct alone, he typed in *'Jake Buchanan'*.

Within seconds, arrest records dominated the screen. Tom clicked on the most recent activity, submitted two days ago.

'Mr Buchanan was photographed leaving his house with suspected drug dealer, Iain Roland at 8.13pm. A young woman, believed to be Elizabeth Archer, the suspect's girl-friend, was seen leaving the premises with them, carrying a rucksack. No clear image of the woman was gained.'

Following this was a grainy photo of Libby leaving with her hood up.

Tom stared at the photo in horror, swearing under his breath.

WE SAT in a nearby coffee shop, trying to get our heads around all that had taken place in the last hour. I was still throbbing with adrenaline and couldn't seem to settle. It was only when Marcus reached across and stilled my hand that I realised I was drumming my fingers on the table.

"Sorry," I mumbled, trying to smile, though it came out as more of a grimace.

Marcus was wearing that intense look of his that I usually loved, but was currently making me feel trapped, like I was a suspect all over again. I was desperately trying to work out why Aneella had drawn the letter S. It was there, frustratingly close to the surface of my memory... yet just out of reach. What had she said to me? *"What did I call him? Think hard, Sophia."*

Damn it to hell! Do you think I'm doing anything but?

I'm failing you all.

The coffee table began to move and shift before me. An odd rushing sound was building in my ears.

"Sophia, I can't help you unless we start talking about it."

His voice seemed to come from far away, even as he was right there before me. My heart began to beat hard, and my face felt clammy and hot. I had to get out of here. Right now.

Abruptly, I stood up, swaying, and Marcus reached out to steady our coffees. Without looking at him, I blurted, "I'll be back," then moved as fast as I could to the ladies' room. The whole time my head was spinning.

Stumbling through the door, I found the nearest cubicle and fell to my knees just in time before the sickness rose up and I retched into the toilet.

After the nausea passed, I flushed the toilet and unsteadily made my way to the sink to wash my face. As I looked up at the mirror, two dark-ringed, anxious eyes stared back at me. Willing me to do better, be stronger. Condemning me for not being so.

MARCUS CRANED his head towards the ladies' toilet for what must have been the eighth time in the last five minutes. He was getting some odd looks from nearby customers sipping their lattes and cappuccinos, but he didn't give a damn. His only thoughts were on how ashen Sophia had looked as she dashed to the toilet.

He'd feared it would prove too much, seeing Aneella. Had he been wrong to push his agenda onto her?

He was seriously contemplating knocking on the door when Sophia emerged, weaving her way slowly back to him. She perched on the edge of the seat, as if about to take flight again, avoiding his eyes as she glanced around, her face pale as a ghost. This alone made Marcus nervous. The last time he'd seen her like that she'd lain bleeding, and he didn't want to relive that moment ever again.

"Are you okay?" he quietly asked her, willing her to look at him.

Sophia finally raised her eyes and he jolted. "I don't feel so good. Is it okay if you take me home before you go back to the office?"

No, was his immediate thought, *it isn't okay, we need to deal with this before it festers.* But after years of dealing with people as a police officer, he knew there was no point pushing when they weren't prepared to open up.

"Aye, I can."

Sophia suddenly reached across to take his hand. "We will talk about it, I promise, but I ... I can't right now."

She looked away again, down at the table. *Why does that cut so deep?* Marcus squeezed her hand, keeping his thoughts to himself.

"Come on, *mo leannan.* Let's get you home."

THE PHONE WAS RINGING INCESSANTLY when Jerry arrived back to his desk, slurping on his nearly cold coffee. He grabbed it, swallowing quickly before rushing out, "Inverness Police. DS Lewis speaking."

There was a pause, with only the sound of quiet breathing.

Frowning, Jerry listened carefully, before saying, "Inverness Police, can I help you?"

Still the same heavy silence. Jerry quickly activated a trace on the caller ID, his suspicions aroused. He knew he only had seconds to take action before the caller hung up.

As predicted, the line went dead. But not before the caller number flashed up on his screen.

As he stared at the caller ID, Jerry found himself swearing under his breath. He knew the number well, all too well.

Marcus was not going to be happy by this news. But then again, not one single part of him was happy about this either.

[11]

The water was calm, without a ripple, and the unusually cloudless sky cast a magnificent indigo reflection, making it almost impossible to tell where the sky ended and the water began.

I sat beside the loch and let its peace settle me. It was strange. Even though this was the loch I'd fallen into a year ago, which could have ended my life there and then, I still found myself coming back to it time and time again. It was as if it held the mystical souls of a thousand Scottish people who'd lived and walked this land I now sat upon. When the mist floated over the water, as it often did, I felt them more keenly still, as if they were calling to me.

Now, I needed them to surround me, help me clear my mind enough to focus on solving this riddle Aneella had given me. What did the S stand for? Why couldn't I remember what she'd called Richard? I was right there the whole time. Surely, she must have said it more than once if she expected me to remember.

I hit the water in frustration, then closed my eyes, letting the breeze cool my burning cheeks.

Almost unconsciously, I laid back on the grass, barely noticing the still-lingering dew seeping through my clothes.

My mind began to flood with the memories I'd long since forced down. They moved like rapid pictures in my head. *Us drinking at the bar, pissed out of our heads. Watching Aneella and Richard slow dance together with a sick feeling in my stomach. Me sitting at the desk in our dorm, surrounded by books, stressed. Looking across to Aneella lying on her bed, laughing into her phone. I don't know who she's talking to but there's flirtation dripping in her voice. I try to block out the sound, turning back to my books, but one or two words still manage to weave their way to me '...so bad, no she won't guess, you sly thing, see you later.'*

There was something of significance in those words, I could almost taste it. But my mind moved on before I could grasp which one.

I'm pushing open the door into our room, laden with books in my arms. I abruptly stop as I'm confronted with Aneella and Richard lying close together on Aneella's bed, Aneella half-clad. They watch me, not moving or drawing back. I stare at them, as if I should feel guilty for intruding. Then Richard lazily moves off the bed and comes up to me. "There you are, darling. You took your time, I almost asked Aneella to come for that drink but she called me an annoying bastard." I look to Aneella, who raises her eyebrows with a bold look, even as she replies to Richard. "You're a sly bastard, a fox scavenging for what he wants." Richard comes up and kisses me on the cheek. Even now I can feel the betrayal in that seemingly innocent kiss.

Then, as if the film reel is cut off, everything goes fuzzy and stops. Squeezing my eyes shut, I focused hard on what I'd heard. The letter S... scavenge.... fox... sly...

With a sudden gasp, I was on my feet, sprinting back to the lodge.

Dear God, let me be right!

. . .

TOM WAITED until lunchtime before he headed out to call Libby, worried if he slipped away before then he would raise suspicion. He stood at the corner where she'd been waiting for him the other evening and felt his stomach knot anxiously as he called her number.

The phone rang and rang, and he was about to hang up, relieved and disappointed, when her voice slurred out, "Hello?"

His first reaction was a physical jolt of desire, which he forced down. The second was more alarming—why the hell did she sound like she was pissed at 1.15 in the afternoon?

The third was the one that hit him full in the gut and made him catch his breath. *I want to take her as far away from here as I can.*

With these conflicting and confusing thoughts racing through him, he didn't immediately respond. Tom heard her repeat herself again, sounding more awake and on edge, "Who's this?"

"Hey, sorry, it's me... Tom."

"Tom? Why've you taken so long? I thought you'd forgotten."

Tom took a breath, then said, "We need to meet. Today."

THE AFTERNOON WAS RAPIDLY DRAWING in, and it left Marcus ever more frustrated. His mind had only been half on his job after reluctantly leaving Soph at their lodge. She'd had a closed-off look as she walked in without so much as a glance at him, something he hadn't seen in a long time. It scared the hell out of him. That, and the fact she'd clearly been sick in the toilet.

The urge to call her had been a hard battle to fight against. But he had succeeded, even if every five minutes he'd been checking his phone to see if she had messaged him. She hadn't.

Now, phone pressed to his ear, he tapped the desk impatiently as he was kept on hold by the Glasgow police department for an eternity. Since they'd found out that the location Tom had pinpointed was a Glasgow address, they had been trying to act fast to get surveillance out there. What they hadn't bargained on was coming across bureaucratic red tape in the shape of Glasgow office with their whole 'this is our area now' bollocks that was frankly annoying the hell out of him. There was no way he was losing this case when they were getting closer. It had consumed too much of him to walk away before being the one to shut down this ring for good.

He was about to lose the will to live if he heard the same monotonous tune a moment longer. Suddenly, a strong Glaswegian voice spoke into his ear. "This is Chief Inspector Jackson. You've been trying to reach me?"

"Aye, I have." Marcus straightened up in his chair, treading carefully. "I don't know how much you know about our ongoing fraud case-"

"I've been brought up to speed."

Marcus raised his eyebrows at the interruption. "Good, good. So, I'm sure you understand why we're keen to get an undercover team in there as soon as possible, preferably in the next few hours. We've already wasted a lot of time."

There was a short pause, making him tense.

"And I'm sure you can understand why we now need to work together on this case, DS Armstrong, as you'd also expect if our roles were reversed. This is now in our jurisdiction."

Marcus swore silently under his breath. This Jackson guy was not going to budge.

"How about this? One or two of your guys join mine on the surveillance team. That way you have direct contact with what's happening on the ground, and we can both act quickly if we need to. But I continue to head this case." Marcus finished, then held his breath, silently counting to ten, a practice he used that never failed to work when questioning suspects.

And this time was no different.

"Aye, I agree to that." Marcus felt the relieved breath come out of him. "But," Jackson continued, "If I'm unhappy with how it's proceeding, I will have no qualms about sending someone to take over, and I'll expect full co-operation."

I won't let it come to that.

"Understood. I appreciate your help in this."

"Good. Get your house in order and close this case. Or I'll be forced to take over and I've got enough shit of my own to deal with."

The phone line went dead. Marcus hung up and rubbed his throbbing forehead. He may have won this battle, but now he was being watched. It wasn't a comfortable feeling.

TWENTY MINUTES LATER, I rushed into Marcus' office. He looked up from his computer, strained.

"Are you okay?"

His face relaxed a little. "Better now that you're less pale than when I last saw you."

I gave an apologetic smile. "I'm sorry I worried you."

Marcus stood and came around to me, taking my face into his hands. I could feel his scrutinising eyes searching mine. This time I held his gaze and whatever he saw there seemed to satisfy my husband. He nodded, giving me a quick kiss. "Aye, well as long as you're okay now."

"Mmm, and better than that," I gave him an excited grin. "I think I've cracked the code name!"

Marcus stared at me, dumbstruck.

I found myself laughing. "Left you speechless? That has to be a first."

Suddenly he gave a loud whoop and lifted me up high. "You wee beauty!"

[12]

As 5:30pm came around, Tom was trying to make a discreet exit to meet Libby when his boss suddenly came out of his office, followed by his wife. Both were looking pleased as punch with themselves. Tom inwardly groaned, feeling trapped. He'd been feeling that way since Libby had pushed her way in and made him act like a deer about to cross the road. He knew he was going to be road-kill but foolishly did it anyway.

Reluctantly, he followed Jerry across to where Marcus stood, sliding a quick glance at his phone. It had taken all his persuasion to get her to meet him in person, rather than tell her over the phone. To hell with that. Aye, she needed to face this.

'Where are u?!' The text screamed at him.

Carefully, he shielded his phone with one hand and quickly shot back, *'Five mins. Stay there!'*

Then he forced himself to tune in to Marcus.

"Thanks, team. As you know, it's been quite frustrating what little progress we've made with this case. Believe me, I feel it more keenly than any of you. But now, Glasgow has agreed to a surveillance on the address we targeted. And after the visit with Ms. Blair today, she has provided us with a clue about the codename used for Mr. Meadows. Following this clue, we think Sophia has figured out the codename." Here, Marcus paused, a small grin on his face as he turned briefly to his wife. "This means we've got an important lead, something that could take us to the ringleader. So, from now on, I want you all focused on picking up on any trails, searches, rhythms, bank accounts, social media accounts, anything that contains the word Slyfox. Everyone got that? I'll repeat just in case: Slyfox. Give me a nod if you got that." Tom and the team nodded. "Good, first thing in the morning, I want you to get straight to it. Leave nothing unturned. If you need to question something then make a note, come to me. Understood? Okay, thanks, team. I'll see you first thing in the morning."

Marcus and Sophia turned away, walking back into his office. Tom saw his chance, and studiously avoiding any kind of eye contact with Jerry, who was looking like he was about to say something, ducked around everyone and headed to the exit. As soon as he was clear, he almost skidded down the stairs, his smooth-soled shoes acting like slippery grease, and practically sprinted out the main front door.

He wondered what the hell he was doing.

CATHY WAS LYING on top of her bed, something she never normally did in the middle of the day. A well-used silver pen was clutched in her hand. A piece of half-written letter, addressed to 'My darling girl' rested on her lap. Her eyes had drifted close a few minutes before, exhaustion biting away at any last reserves she still hung onto.

She didn't know how long she'd slept like the living

dead. All she knew, when her consciousness finally dragged her awake, something had shifted in the air, as if it had been holding its breath all this time, waiting for her.

Something was screaming at her not to leave the room. But pushing it away, telling herself not to be so silly, Cathy tenderly put the letter and pen to one side and slowly stood. Her bones ached to the joint. Rubbing her lower back in a circular motion, she moved out of her bedroom and onto the slightly creaking landing.

Nothing stirred.

Everything within her felt as if it was suspended, held tight. As she carefully made her way downstairs, she already knew the truth. What emotional cost awaited her.

She forced herself to go on, one step followed by the other until she was in the room where he lay. At first, everything seemed as it normally was and had been since that fatal stroke had cruelly taken away the active life he once took for granted, and with it robbing her of her husband.

But as she came softly up to him, she knew instinctively her Derek was gone, his spirit finally released from the body that had been his prison. His eyes were half open, half shut. They no longer searched for her, trying to speak a thousand words that could never be uttered.

Cathy reached out and tentatively touched his cheek. It was icy cold. She took a shocked step back, then raised a hand to cover her mouth and stifle a cry.

It took her a few moments of breathing hard, before she could once more stretch out her shaking hand to touch him, then gently close his eyelids for the last time. This time she didn't, couldn't, hold back the emotion erupting within her. It felt like everything was shattering within her.

She pressed her brow against his, tears wetting both their cheeks, cradling his face as she had done for the last forty years. "You're free now, my darling, you're free. Godspeed, my dear, godspeed my sweet darling love. I'll join you soon. But I can't leave our girl yet."

She pressed her lips to his leathery skin forehead, and let her heart bleed out, as the darkness closed in around her.

THE AIR BIT at him as he raced around the corner to where she was meant to be, the same place where she'd originally waited for him, near the tree.

When Tom saw her pacing nervously and looking anxiously up and down the street, something shuddered painfully within him. But there was no way he going to allow himself to dwell on that. Instead, he came up to her, noting how she hugged herself against the wind in another barely-there top. "Libby."

The speed in which she spun around nearly sent them both sprawling to the ground. He reached out to steady them both. She grasped his arm, staring up at him in fear. What was it about those haunted brown eyes of hers that got to him every time? "Easy there," he murmured. "Alright?"

Her eyes turned from frightened to stormy in a millisecond. "Bloody hell! Don't creep up on me like that! And where the hell have you been?!"

"I didn't think I was creeping up on you," Tom mildly responded, ignoring her second question. Seeing her eyes narrow, he decided to swiftly move the conversation on. "Listen, we need to go somewhere more private so we can talk. Let's go this way." *Away from the station.*

Grabbing her hand so she had no choice but to follow him, Tom led them to Fraser Park a few blocks away, Libby protesting all the way. To his relief, only a few dog walkers and determined mums with protesting toddlers were around, everyone else no doubt put off by the grey, overcast day.

"Would you quit dragging me some! What's got into you?"

Libby was trying to free her hand from his vice grip. Knowing he had pushed his luck enough, Tom pulled them over to a bench to sit down. Only then did he release her. She immediately began rubbing her hand. "I thought you would be the one person who wouldn't hurt me." Her head was slightly turned away as she said that, and it took Tom a few seconds to process what she said.

Frowning, he quietly said as a fire burned darkly within him, "Someone's hurting you?"

"Apart from you, you mean?"

"Aye, apart from me. And you know I wasn't intentionally doing so. I wanted to make sure I didn't lose you."

Libby gave him a withering look. "Yeah, that's what he says too. Look," she hurried on as Tom went to open his mouth, "Forget all that, alright? It doesn't matter. Just tell me what you've found out."

Although she was trying to appear brazen and tough, he wasn't fooled. Having been near her for so long, drinking in every look, every mannerism of hers, Tom knew her better than he knew himself. Right now, she was scared shitless. And for every good reason.

Tom reached into his trouser pockets and pulled out a crumpled piece of paper folded in four. Libby stared at it, then him. "What's that?"

"When I checked out your name, there was nothing against it."

Relief swam in her eyes, and she gave a rare smile. It made him feel like a heel. Before he lost his nerve, Tom blurted out, "But your name comes up with Jake's name."

Her tentative smile slipped. "That bastard's got a criminal record and now he's got your name associated with his." He shook his head, dark anger stirring within him. "Here, see for yourself."

He handed her the piece of paper. Libby's hands trembled as she reluctantly took the paper and unfolded it. Then her eyes collided with his – her fear drowned them both.

[13]

The streets of Glasgow were their usual busy hive as I crossed from Glasgow Bridge into the centre itself. It wasn't a city I was familiar with, and the imposing gothic-style buildings and fast pace of the passing pedestrians added to the urge to walk as quickly as I could to meet Marcus, who was visiting someone at the Glasgow police station.

My mind was full of the meeting I had just had with the client of a bank I had worked for before. This man, Mr. Rogers, was someone new to me, and I wasn't in a hurry to meet with him again. Something in his probing manner and penetrating eyes had unsettled me.

I'd been shown into a smart-looking office. Mr Rogers had stood up from behind his desk and indicated for me to sit on one of two chairs. He came and sat uncomfortably close beside me as I pulled out my laptop. I tried not to feel flustered, forcing myself to take a deep, steadying breath.

Once I had the mock-up program in front of us, I relaxed a little as I talked him through the program I was recommending for his bank, keeping my eyes fixed on my laptop the whole time to avoid having to look up.

"So, as you can see, this will help you run your accounts more efficiently, with accurate up to the minute details on transactions taking place, which was your requirement for this program."

I finally had no option but to look up. Mr. Rogers was still looking at me. A hot flush went up over me again and my voice was a little hesitant as I said, "Is everything ... satisfactory to what you were looking for?"

There was long bated pause. "Ms. Meadows, or should I say Mrs. Armstrong... is your program susceptible to bank fraud?

That threw me, utterly. Did he *know*? But how? That was impossible! The case hadn't made it to court yet. I tried to keep my voice neutral as I said, "Is that something you're concerned about?

Mr Rogers gave a bland smile. "Concerned ... and interested."

I knew I was staring open-mouthed, trying and failing to look unruffled, while inside my stomach twisted into a tight knot.

"I assure you, I put in firewalls to protect my programs at all costs."

"I'm sure you do, Ms. Meadows. But nothing is one-hundred-percent foolproof, is it?"

He leaned forward. Instinctively I moved back, frowning.

"No, no of course not. There's always a very small possibility a program can fall into the wrong hands. No programmer can one-hundred-percent guarantee it, Mr. Rogers. If they did, they would leave themselves open to be sued."

He laughed. "Don't look so worried, Ms. Meadows! I'm

merely asking the questions they'll ask me. It's occurred to me as we've been speaking that programmers are in the perfect position to commit fraud by selling their programs to the highest bidder."

This made me physically baulk. "I'm sorry?" I managed to force out, all the while my mind whirring rapidly as I tried to work out how the hell he knew.

Mr. Rogers grinned, clearly enjoying my discomfort. "It's an intriguing idea, isn't it? I do wonder if you are as surprised by my statement as you make out. The drive of money can turn any of us into criminals. Perhaps you've even considered it yourself?"

That cool steely gaze continued until my own had no choice but to look away. I hated my timidity in that moment, more than I ever had before. I should defend myself. Why the hell was I taking this from him?

You know why.

Feeling faint, I murmured. "Maybe you'd like to come back to me when you've made a decision."

Quickly, wanting to get out, I closed down the laptop and hastily stood up, avoiding Mr. Rogers's eyes as he continued to grin.

"How fascinating you haven't denied it, Ms. Meadows. Which begs the question, should I trust you?"

I left without saying another word.

Now, as I walked hurriedly through the streets, checking on my maps app to see if I was heading in the right direction, the almost sickening smell of his aftershave still lingered on me, making me feel a little nauseous. That and the disturbing, disbelieving thought Mr. Rogers somehow knew my codes had already been used for fraud. I couldn't quite shake the feeling, the cold shudder creeping down my spine, that it was so.

My phone beeped, alerting me to a text. I looked down while I carried on walking and felt my spirits lift in seeing Marcus' name flash up. 'Wrapping up the meeting – can't come soon enough. Where are you? xxx'

I went to reply, only to realise I had no clue where I was. I glanced up and frowned. I must have turned too soon, as I was now standing in a dark, enclosed alleyway, blocked by the sunlight. I shivered in the lurking shadows. Flipping up the map app to try to work out where the hell I was, I was met with a weak, intermittent signal. I swore under my breath.

Suddenly, the hairs on the back of my neck stood up and fear enveloped me, overriding every other emotion.

I was being followed.

I remembered this stomach-churning, heart pounding feeling after that low-time criminal Daryl, paid by Lyle, had followed me last year. Only this time, this was a complete stranger, an opportunist.

Slowly, my breath coming out in quick, shallow breaths, I looked over my shoulder discreetly. A man, his face concealed by a hood, was within a few metres of me, coming close.

Too close.

Acting instinctively, fear shooting through me, I ran as quickly as I could. All the while, I was aware I was being further and further trapped in the alleyway, with no obvious route of escape.

Hating this petrifying feeling of vulnerability, yet unable to dispel it from me, I did the only thing I could think of: call Marcus. Yet, as my shaking hand went to do so, I was suddenly jerked back so hard I nearly fell over. My scream filled the stagnant air as my backpack was yanked off my shoulder.

"No, stop!" I cried out as I clung on to it as hard as I could. His sleeve jerked up to reveal a dagger tattoo on his wrist.

I never saw the hit. But the immediate pain, I felt that. As everything blurred around me, I was vaguely aware of the figure running off with my backpack before everything went dark.

[14]

S omething was wrong, he could feel it.

The air had turned bitterly cold suddenly. Marcus felt the biting wind as he once more tried Sophia's mobile from where he stood outside the Glasgow police station. Once again it rang out. It wasn't like her. She always picked up, no matter what, even if she cursed him for calling at the wrong time.

Thank God they both had a locator app on their phones. He opened the app and clicked on her face. It zoomed in on a street he had never heard of. She had been there in the same location for twenty minutes. Too long, way too long to be standing still.

"Shit," he muttered, "Shit!" He quickly typed the address into his maps. Then he began to run, hard.

IT WAS the cold hardness of the pavement pressed against my cheek that slowly seeped into my consciousness. My eyes reluctantly opened and tried frantically to make sense of where I was. Everything was hazy, funny, like a camera aperture on the wrong setting. I raised my hand to try and clear them, only to stare at the dried-up, reddish stain on them. Was that blood? Why was there blood?

I went to lift my head. A sharp pain ripped through me, and I cried out in shock. Dizziness had me closing my eyes again, as once more I drifted off...

HE WAS CLOSE. *How the hell did she end up here? What was she thinking?!*

Marcus, his eyes burning holes into his phone as he constantly checked on the map app, came running round the corner, nearly knocking over a hunched-up woman pulling her trolley, who began cursing him with language that would make his mother blush. No time to stop and apologise.

He skidded to a stop as his phone told him he had arrived at his destination. *What the-*

It was a dark, dismal alleyway with towering walls that seemed to close in on him. His eyes scrunched up tight as he tried to adjust to the deepening gloom, desperately trying to see.

Then his heart stopped.

She was lying on the ground, face pressed against the pavement, still. Far, far too still.

"Sophia..." his voice came out in a whisper, as if his voice had been strangled. A flashback of her lying like this once before almost had him buckling.

Then he was falling to his knees, automatically checking first for breath—thank God, she was breathing—then for injuries, running his hand gently over her. When it came away with blood from a wound on the back of her head, he felt his stomach heave and coldness creep over him. He bent his head close to hers, as he stroked her cheek.

"Sophia, Sophia, lass, wake up now. Come on, *mo leannan*, wake up for me."

IT WAS the sound of his voice, a voice that I knew as intimately as my own, that brought me back. I opened my eyes, saw his concerned ones looking down at me, and gave a soft, dreamy smile.

"I knew you would find me. You always find me."

"Always, *mo leannan*, always," came his thickened reply.

IT WAS MUCH LATER when we were finally home. I had flatly refused to stay in the hospital after they had done a CT scan and found no internal bleeding or undue concerns. I couldn't stay there—the thought of it brought me close to panic. I had already lost too many months in a ward. Marcus hadn't been happy, but there must have been something in my eyes that stopped him from arguing, and instead he had merely nodded.

I laid in bed with a banging headache and an overwhelming need to sleep and pretended none of it had happened. Once again, I had become a victim, unable to protect myself, and I hated, *hated* that. More than the injury, more than losing my laptop—thank god it was only a backup one—more than even the fact I could have died, was that I had been helpless. All my old insecurities and doubts were trying to bury me.

I must have given a soft groan, for Marcus came rushing in, looking strained - a look I had caused far too many times.

"Are you okay? Do you need some more tablets?"

I shook my head, tried to smile. "No, it's okay, I'll take some more later."

Marcus came and sat down, causing the mattress to shift. "We'll need to take your statement tomorrow, when you're ready."

"I don't remember much."

"Whatever you can remember will help, trust me. I'm coming with you, no arguments," he added, giving me a stern look.

"Actually, I would prefer it if you were there," I admitted, reaching for his hand, which he clasped in his, bringing it briefly to his lips.

"Thank god that wasn't your main laptop. Aye, the last thing we need is your codes being stolen again." He shook his head at the thought.

I frowned, staring at him. Marcus gave me a funny look. "What are you thinking?"

My words came out carefully. "The meeting I had beforehand, with Mr. Rogers, was odd. He kept making comments about my codes being susceptible to fraud... as if he knew and wanted to see whether I could be persuaded to sell them."

"And then you were followed, and only the laptop was taken, not your handbag or phone... which means it wasn't a random attack," Marcus finished.

We looked at one another, seeing the dawning truth in the other's eyes.

He was coming... he was coming for me. With my heart beating wildly, I spun around as the walls moved ever in, enclosing me, darkness extinguishing the last of the light. I could feel him within a hair's breadth. I tried to scream but no sound came out. No, *no,* I moaned in silent fear, frantically trying to push back, only to encounter hard stone as my head cracked against it. His eyes were glittering in the dark and his hand was reaching for me, trapping me, imprisoning me. "You can't escape me, Soph. You never will." Grinning wildly, Richard bent his head towards me—

I sat bolt upright, panting hard, my pulse dangerously high, my skin cold with shivering sweat. Bile burned my throat. I had to get out of here. Now. I half-stumbled, half-ran through the lodge, dragged the door open and leaned heavily on the railing outside. Taking large gulps of air, I squeezed my eyes shut and desperately tried to erase the image of Richard's dangerous, cold eyes, hellbent on destroying me.

I can't go on like this...

THE LIGHT WAS BARELY BREAKING through the denseness of the night when Marcus stirred, stretching out to find the sheet cold beside him. Jumping up so fast his head spun, he stumbled out of the bedroom and scanned the lounge and kitchen. She wasn't there. Beginning to panic, he called out her name. No answer.

It was then he noticed the front door ajar. Grabbing a blanket, he walked outside and found her, staring out as she held on to the wooden veranda, shivering a little in a thin camisole. She looked as pale as the moonlight that covered her.

Coming up behind her, Marcus covered her with the blanket. She immediately jerked back, turning wildly on him. Her blind fear made his breath catch in trepidation. He forced his voice to be as calm as possible as he gently placed the blanket around her shoulders. "Ach, you gave me a surprise, waking up to find you not there. Come back inside now, where it's warmer."

Sophia stared through him, as if he wasn't there, before turning away from him.

"Soph?" he said.

The minutes ticked by, with her far away from him. He felt helpless.

When she at last moved her head back to him, something had changed within her. There was a set to her jaw, a new determination in her eyes as they bore hard into his. "I want you to teach me self-defence, Marcus. I want you to show me how to protect myself."

She came up close to him, pressing her hands on his chest.

There was fire in her voice as she said, "I am done being a victim."

[15]

"Ms. Blair, you've got a call. Would you like to come and accept it?"

The firm tone left no room for argument despite its suggested choice. Aneella stood from where she had been seated in the common room, wiping her suddenly sweaty palms down her trousers. As she followed the prison officer down the cool corridor, a chill began to move down her spine. A pressure began to build around her heart, like a rock wedged within.

They entered a room, with a phone and nothing else, stripped to the core and as soulless as it could get.

The prison officer picked up the phone, murmured into it then turned and pointed it towards Aneella.

Everything within her screamed not to take it. The prison officer began to tut.

"Ms Blair, your caller is waiting."

Swallowing, Aneella finally stepped forward and took it with a shaking hand. "Hello?" she forced out.

At the sound of her mother's grief-stricken voice breaking, as Cathy tried to find the words to tell her daughter the heartbreaking news, the rock grew larger within her, until her chest heaved with the effort of breathing, and every intake was painful. Her eyes squeezed shut against the tide threatening to drown her. She slowly crumpled to the floor, hugging her knees, letting the phone fall away while the sound of her mother's sobbing echoed off the walls.

Her father was dead.

And she had failed him. She had failed him.

I WAS TRYING to ignore the persistent headache I'd had since the mugging four days ago. As the Scottish air was being kind and warmer than average for autumn, I had set myself up on the veranda to work. But my heart wasn't in it, and instead, I kept looking out over the loch and almost dozing off.

Rubbing my tired eyes, I tried once again to focus. Marcus had agreed to start my self-defence training later, and I wasn't letting anything put him off doing this. I wanted, no, I *needed* to take control. The nightmares had only increased in their intensity, merging, evolving between this recent one and my previous attack, but always with Richard coming after me.

I had given my statement to a bored-looking police officer back in Glasgow. I wasn't surprised he had been less than enthused by my written statement—I barely remembered any details. Marcus, however, had blown up a storm and told the poor officer his superior would be hearing from him. To be honest, I was surprised no actual steam came out of Marcus' ears, he was that riled up by the lack of professionalism. The police officer had 'woken up' then, looking more than a little petrified. I'd felt sorry for him and urged a still fuming Marcus out of there.

The phone beside me came to life. I reached down with a start and frowned when I saw who the caller was.

"Hello. How are you?"

There was a brief overwhelming silence. Then I heard a soft cry that pierced my heart. "Sophia dear? It's me, Cathy. I—I'm afraid I have some sad news. It's about my Derek..."

AFTER TWENTY MINUTES and the promise to visit as soon as possible, I let my phone drop away, trying to fight the tears threatening to overcome me, ones I'd held back from the moment I heard her break down. All I kept picturing was the last time I'd seen him, and the tender love in her eyes as she'd tended to him. He'd been released, at least, from the prison his mind had been trapped in. Still, it was so achingly hard for Cathy. And Aneella. *Oh, Ella...* I knew she was hurting badly. Cathy had said she hadn't been allowed to tell Aneella in person, that her daughter had been far too silent on the phone, barely saying a word. Of course, that's exactly what Aneella would do—shut herself away and pretend she was fine. But inside... inside she must have been breaking up. I had seen it once, only once, before, when her dad suffered a catastrophic stroke—a rare glimpse into a heart that seemed to beat without emotion.

But should I go see her again?

Do I have it in me?

Did I even have a choice in this? The right thing to do was plain, and I couldn't ignore it... or her.

God, will I ever be free of her?

"SHOW ME AGAIN," I bit out in frustration, sweat pouring off me and my head pounding. We were outside by the loch and Marcus had been showing me some basic front kicks. The only difference was that he was barely sweating, fit from ten years of kickboxing and a mixed martial arts background, whereas I was practically heaving my guts up, and my breath was coming out in sharp gasps.

Marcus stood there with his hands on his hips, his forehead creased in concern. I was beginning to resent that look. Dammit, I was so tired of everyone looking at me like that.

"One more time, then we're stopping for today."

"No! I—"

He stepped up to me and put his hands firmly on my shoulder. "You've never done anything like this before, and we need to build up your stamina and fitness levels. Listen to me, *mo leannan*, I know what I'm doing. We're going to mix this up with basic kickboxing moves and self-defence, along with HIT-"

"We're going to hit each other?"

Marcus laughed. "Well, no doubt you'll get the joy of hitting me soon. But no, I mean high-impact training and cardio."

He laughed again when he saw my face and spread his hands wide. "You asked me to train you, right?"

"Yes, dammit it to hell, I did," I muttered, shaking out my tired muscles.

"Remember why you are doing this. Keep focused on that. One more time, let's do this."

I won't be a victim anymore.

My body reset itself into the stance we had been practising, left foot forward, knees slightly bent, and begin to do front kicks, one, two, keep on repeating for ten, change to the other leg...

. . .

MUCH LATER, after we shared a bath, where most of the water had ended up outside the tub as Marcus had worked his magic hands over my aching muscles, then a late supper, I finally got around to telling him about Derek. He immediately sat up from his previously slouched position and a thousand thoughts seemed to race over his eyes as the detective in him switched into gear.

"My heart broke for her, she sounded so lost and devastated," I said, hugging a mug of coffee in my hands. "I think I'll pop 'round with some flowers tomorrow. I know it's a release in one way, she lost him in so many ways years ago. But it's still a shock when it happens..."

I turn to my husband, aware I was treading on sensitive areas with him caring for his late wife, Lucy. I was prepared to see that haunted look in his eyes I'd known all too well. Instead, he seemed... distracted, looking into the distance.

I waved my hand in front of him to bring him back to me. "Hello? Earth to Marcus. Are you hearing anything I'm saying?"

He gave a little start then finally turned to me, giving an apologetic half-smile. "Aye, aye I am. And you're right, the shock and all never prepares you for it, no matter how much you think you are. The grief just lies stagnant within you, with nowhere to go. It's the worst kind of emotion because it drains your very soul."

He shook his head, as if to shake the grief out of him. Without a word, I put down the mug and put my arms around his neck, pulling him tight against me, holding him close. His arms wrapped around me, his head dropping into the space between my shoulder and the curve of my neck. We stayed like that for a long moment, then I felt his mouth gently press a kiss against the sensitive skin of my neck before pulling back. I felt the loss of his warmth immediately, as I always did.

I reached for my coffee and as I took a sip, I became aware I was being watched intently. I raised my eyebrows. "Feeling a little like a 'suspect under scrutiny' again. We've talked about this. Wife does not like."

There was a moment of silence while he continued to stare at me with an excitement dancing in his eyes, as the cogs in his brain went into overdrive.

I felt myself tense in anticipation.

Marcus said, "Aneella must be feeling very vulnerable and alone right now, grieving the loss of her father and all that. So therefore, more amenable to talk with us perhaps, aye?"

I gaped, hardly believing those words had come out of his mouth. Then I stood up and walked away with a shake of my head, slamming the bedroom door behind me when my husband exclaimed in protest. "What did I say?"

[16]

There had been a definite chill around the house the following morning, and it wasn't due to the cool autumn air swirling in, lingering over the loch like a fine mist. His wife was not talking to him. That was something he hadn't experienced before.

At work, Marcus sighed and rubbed his jaw as he sat at his desk. He didn't get it. It was mostly down to Sophia that Aneella was in prison awaiting trial. It was because of Aneella, and Richard, that his wife still suffered. So why wouldn't she want him to press in on Aneella while she was at her most vulnerable so they could find that bastard, Richard? But no, apparently he was the bastard for even thinking about using Aneella while she was grieving.

Yet every instinct was screaming at him not to let this perfect opportunity pass by. Which meant he had to think of some way to talk Sophia into seeing this his way.

He groaned, blowing out a breath.

There was a rap on his door. Marcus looked up and smiled at Tom.

"Don't stand there catching flies, come in, take a pew."

Tom gave a faint smile and did as bidden, sitting down in the chair opposite. Marcus found himself properly looking at his young sergeant for the first time in a while. Something was missing in the young man – what was it? There was a slight slump to the shoulders and eyes that no longer held their usual spark. It hit him – Tom had lost his youthful cheekiness. When the hell had that happened? Seeing this bit hard at Marcus. He didn't want Tom to be growing jaded or losing his sense of who he was.

Marcus leaned forward, giving his habitual frown. "How are you doing there, young Tom? Ach, I'm sorry I've not had much chance to support you. That's my bad. You know you can come to me anytime, tell me anything that's bothering you?"

Tom's eyes widened. "What makes you think anything is bothering me?"

Marcus gave a small smile. "I don't have many talents, but one I do have is being able to read people. I'm reading you right now and know something is weighing on your mind. So why don't you tell me what it is."

It wasn't a question, but an expectation that Tom would share. He swallowed hard against the need to explode that was burning within him. Libby was putting pressure on him. She was scared as shit and he was in an impossible position, where there was no right way out.

He stared at his boss, a man he admired. There weren't many of those. His father was a raging alcoholic who barely held down a job, his uncle a waste of space, a lazy leeching sod who fed off society without putting anything back into it, and Tom was embarrassed by them both. He'd carefully hidden his family from his team, and likewise, his family didn't even know he worked for the force. He missed his mam. She deserved better, a hell of a lot better than what she had been 'blessed' with, and he sent her money to a secret bank account only she knew about so she could at least get some decent food inside her. He had grown up in Glasgow—the rough side—and as soon as he was able, Tom got out of there as fast as he could. Inverness seemed like a holiday in comparison.

But it seemed that crap was determined to follow him against his best efforts, and his promising police career seemed already up the shit creek. That bleak thought had him swallowing again and looking away to control his emotions. He could feel Marcus' steady eyes on him, not giving an inch of reprieve. How could he phrase it without raising suspicion? He forced himself to look back at Marcus.

"Is there ... is there ever a way a file could simply ... vanish?"

His boss looked startled for a moment before rear-ranging his features into a neutral expression. "You mean deleted?"

"Aye, aye, deleted, wiped," Tom nodded quickly.

Marcus paused. "In theory, any a police officer who has access to the database could delete a file. But by doing so they would trigger an immediate alert for suspicious behaviour and be under investigation. Only juveniles have their records cleared at the age of eighteen. Any adult over the age of eighteen who has been convicted will perma-nently remain on our database."

"What if they hadn't been convicted but are only under suspicion?" Tom was grasping at straws, praying that if Libby stayed out of suspicion, she could simply 'disap-pear'... only for his hope to be crushed when Marcus shook his head firmly.

"Same rules." He leaned forward across the desk. "Tom,

I would have thought they had taught you all of this when you were at training school. Is there something you've seen that's concerned you? If so, you can tell me."

God, I wish I could.

MARCUS WATCHED his young sergeant retreat into his persona as he plastered on his happy-go-lucky smile, and told Marcus he was only asking out of interest. But he wasn't fooled for a minute. Something was eating away at this young lad, and he could only hope that sometime soon Tom would confide in him. A sudden dark fear gripped him, making his chest grow tight. It was all too easy to be corrupted by the underworld lurking at the young and vulnerable police officers along with the jaded, bitter older officers. Marcus had seen its poison seep into one of his own officers, Andy, and the pain of that betrayal still cut deep. *Don't let it take this one too.*

But now was not the right time to push it.

"So, have you had any breakthrough with the codename 'Slyfox'?"

The immediate relief on Tom's face with the change of topic was so striking, it left a sharp sinking feeling inside him.

"Aye, good, good. It's why I came in to see you." Tom leaned forward excitedly opening his file he'd been clutching in his hands. He handed Marcus a printout of text messages, each containing 'Slyfox' somewhere in the body of the text. "As you can see, all these messages we've traced have this name in them. The messages are in code, which we need to decipher, but it all seems to be coming from the same number."

Marcus felt a shiver of excitement as he scanned over the page. "And do we have a recipient of the texts?"

Tom pointed to one of the numbers. "This one seems to be appearing the most, though they never reply. Is that a wee bit odd that they're not?"

"Replying?" Marcus shook his head. "No, these phones tend to be burner phones, using pay-as-you-go cards and used to a minimum. This is good work, well done. Keep seeing if we can decode them and get a pinpoint on the location the texts are being sent from. I've got a gut feeling it may be in or near the Glasgow flat we've already got under surveillance."

"Thanks, Boss." Tom grinned, looking more like himself. Marcus smiled back, feeling absurdly happy to hear Tom call him 'Boss'.

"Can you ask Jerry to come see me? Thanks, Tom."

WHEN THE PRISON OFFICER, a sour-faced woman who clearly wasn't getting any satisfaction, jobwise or any other kind, came to her cell and told her she had a visitor, a small, triumphant smile lingered over Aneella's lips as she stood up to follow. She knew Sophia wouldn't be able to stay away. No matter that it was because of her that Aneella found herself locked up. She was like a drug to Sophia, an addiction she would always crave, like a fly drawn to a spider's web... and Aneella relished the power that she possessed.

The fluorescent light on the corridor flickered annoyingly overhead as they walked silently down the corridor to the visitor area, with only the squeak of the warden's trainers along the floor breaking it.

Aneella was anticipating what Sophia would say, how she could sweet-talk Sophia back into her bidding once again. Her grin grew wider as a thrill she hadn't felt in a long time coursed through her, waking her from a deathly slumber.

They rounded a corner. Aneella caught a glimpse of auburn hair sitting at the table, and eagerly stepped around... only to freeze in utter shock.

"What the hell are you doing here?" she burst out.

I WAS STILL FUMING a few hours later. My husband had wisely left me in peace. He hadn't got why I was so upset at the idea of using Aneella or why I felt like boxing him between his eyes with one of the new punches he'd taught me. No one, whether an angel or a devil in disguise, should be used at their most vulnerable state. No matter what they had done.

And perhaps there was still a small, unacknowledged part of me that cared for her, despite every betrayal.

I sighed as I put the food shopping away. No doubt he would want to talk it out later, and I really didn't have the energy for it. I had been feeling a little off-colour all day. When would this cursed headache ever let up? My hand gingerly touched the back of my head where I'd been hit, and I flinched a little. I closed my eyes against the sudden nausea that hit me.

As I took in deep, gulping breaths, my mobile rang. I looked across as it vibrated loudly on my worktop, wanting to ignore it.

Then I saw 'caller unknown' and my stomach heaved violently. I rushed to the sink just in time, then dragged a cloth against my mouth as my gaze went unwittingly back to the phone. It stopped, then immediately started vibrating again, demanding attention.

I knew exactly who it was, as impossible it should have been for him to have my ex-directory phone number, which had been changed after the attack.

My ex-husband.

JERRY WAS SITTING HUNCHED over his computer, trying to decide if he should tell Marcus his suspicions or not. All he had was a sixth sense that it was Andy calling into the station here. But why? And what the hell did he want all of a sudden?

The pain of his ex-colleague's betrayal still cut deep.

He saw again the last time Andy had been here. It had been the day they had arrested Ms. Blair, and everything had exploded into action.

Jerry had been standing watching from a distance as Andy sat at his desk. He had been watching Andy for a while. Something had changed within the man he'd considered not only a colleague but a friend. Andy had always been a live wire, though tried to taper it down at work. Somehow every beer they'd gone out for had ended in a near bar brawl and too many times to count Jerry had had to get Andy out of them before he got both their heads kicked in. It was like there was a restlessness in Andy that never quite got satisfied.

Yet in those last few weeks leading up to that day, there was a new edginess to him. He had become uncharacteristically secretive, disappearing off without explanation. And against his personal desire to believe the best of a friend, Jerry's trained police skills kicked into life, and told him to watch every move.

That afternoon last year, as they waited for a tense

Marcus to get Ms. Blair to the interview room, Andy was putting his phone down, ending a call. He had looked sweaty, pulling at his collar uncomfortably, shifting in his seat before standing up just as Jerry walked over towards his desk. As he did, he glanced a look at Andy's computer. The computer was on lock screen.

Andy looked across at Jerry, and gave a forced laugh, "Ssh, don't tell the boss man, but I'm sneaking out for a wee drink. Be back shortly."

Jerry frowned. "We are going to be needed when Marcus interviews Ms. Blair."

"Sure, sure. I'll be back."

Andy grinned, though it didn't reach his eyes, then swiftly turned, and walked out of the bull pit area, disappearing out of sight.

It was the last time Jerry saw him.

Later that day, Andy left a message saying he was sick and couldn't come back in, which in the craziness no one saw till next day. Then after a few days and still no sign of him back from 'sick leave' Jerry had tried calling but the number was disconnected. Marcus, off himself while Sophia recovered, had told Jerry to pass it up to HR, which he'd done.

But all this time, something had never sat right about it and left him with an uncomfortable feeling in the pit of his stomach.

"Hey Jerry, boss wants to see you in his office."

He swung his head up at the sound of young Tom, as he was nicknamed.

"Aye okay, thanks."

Jerry heaved himself out of the chair, still mulling it over, as he entered Marcus' office, momentarily taken aback to find Marcus leaning on his desk, instead of his habitual place behind it or standing by the window looking out over the city below.

"Sir?"

Marcus swung his head up, his eyes glazed before clearing with a blink. So many times, Jerry wondered what thoughts took his boss far away. One thing was certain, Jerry sure didn't envy him his job, and the crippling responsibility that came with it.

"Jerry. I know I ask a lot of you—"

"Nothing I can't handle. I would tell you if I couldn't."

Marcus gave a faint smile. "That's good to hear. Since Andy left without warning, and with Tom too wet behind the ears to handle more complex matters, I'm afraid it's going to keep falling on you 'til we find a replacement." He pulled a face. "God knows when that will be."

This was his perfect moment to voice his suspicions. Jerry went to speak but caught up in his own thoughts, Marcus ploughed on without noticing as he began to pace the room.

"What I'm going to say is in the strictest confidence, aye?" Marcus stopped, looking directly at him. Jerry nodded. Marcus nodded in reply then continued, speaking quite rapidly. "Sophia was mugged a few days ago when we were in Glasgow. She was hit over the head and her laptop was stolen."

Jerry stared, appalled at his boss, stepping closer. "Is she okay? Was she..."

"Aye, mostly so, just a lingering headache." Marcus turned and looked directly at him, swallowing hard, a look of lingering worry darkening his eyes.

"Good, good," Jerry breathed out, "Sophia sure as hell doesn't deserve this, she's been through so much already."

"That she has."

There was a quiet moment, both caught up in their

thoughts when Jerry quietly said, "Was it a random attack, a case of wrong time, wrong place?"

Marcus hesitated, the silence dragging out, before "I don't believe that it was." As Jerry digested this, he continued. "Sophia had left a meeting with a potential bank client, who seemed to hint that he knew her computer codes had been used for a fraud. It hasn't even made it to court yet, so there is no way he should have known. Immediately after, she was followed and mugged." He paused. "She had her phone and her handbag containing money and credit cards, all of that, yet only her laptop was taken."

"Nothing else?"

Marcus shook his head. "Nothing."

They both looked at each other, understanding exactly what that meant. Too many obvious coincidences already triggering alarm bells. It was what they had been trained to look for.

"You want me to put some feelers out on this bank client?" Jerry asked, already knowing the answer.

"Damn right I do." There was an angry fire in Marcus' eyes. "I don't trust those eejits working at Glasgow station. I want to know exactly who this Mr. Rogers is and what game he's playing. No one hurts my wife and gets away with it."

[17]

The nights were drawing in fast as autumn came.

A cool breeze stirred the recently fallen leaves around our feet as Marcus bent down to kiss my rain-splattered forehead. "I'm sorry."

I closed my eyes and leaned into him with a soft sigh, letting him envelope me. I could never stay angry at Marcus for long. And it had been one horrible, hellish day. I really needed to feel his unwavering strength right then. "I'm sorry too," I breathed out.

We stayed like that until the soft rain turned more persistent and, laughing, we sprinted inside, our clothes drenched and plastered to our skin. We fell into each other, giggling.

Stripping first, Marcus gave me a lingering grin as I struggled to get my own wet jeans off, before unceremoniously pushing me back onto the sofa. He yanked off one leg of the jeans, then the other, followed by my knickers, jumper, and bra, all flying off in different directions. The glint in his eye matched my own and I hungrily pulled him over me, wanting to feel him take me completely, give him everything I have. I could feel his hardness pressed against me as I rocked underneath him, hear him moan softly as my teeth gently bit his shoulder, my hands clenching his ass. He moved down my body, using his mouth to make my skin tingle, before taking my nipple in his mouth as his fingers moved between my legs, finding my wetness and driving me to thrust against his hand, wanting more. Just as I was close to coming, I suddenly found myself flipped over so my stomach was pressed against the cushions. His mouth was on my back, moving tantalisingly down before stopping.

"Marcus!" I gasped, reaching around to feel for him as he hovered over me, his breath on my neck.

"Tell me what you want," he murmured, rubbing himself against my ass.

"You, I want … you." I strained my neck back to pull him into a kiss. He flipped me over and cupped my breasts before moving down to slightly raise my hips and part my thighs, then with one thrust, he was at last inside me. I was close to coming and moved with him urgently until at last we both climaxed together, shuddering hard, bathed in sweat, and sated.

LATER, curled up against him with my back pressed against his chest, it was on the tip of my tongue to tell him about the repeated calls I'd so cowardly avoided answering, I swear that it was. I should have told him all of it: the emails, Richard having my phone number, my plan to draw him out by using myself as bait.

How I would bitterly regret my decision that night. But in that moment, I naively thought that tomorrow I would call Richard and arrange a meeting somewhere public, and it would all come to a quick ending.

How wrong I could be.

TOM WAS SLUMPED on the sofa with a beer in hand, watching some TV program about a woman in search of a missing person with only a grainy photo to help her, when there was a knock on the door. He was tempted to leave it but seeing as his flatmate was in the next room and already shouting at them to get lost, Tom rolled his eyes and heaved himself up to open it.

She was standing there in the gloom of the hallway, already putting her hand out towards him as if she thought he was about to slam the door on her.

"What are you doing here?" he blurted out before he could consider his words.

"What, I don't even get an invite in now?" Libby commented sarcastically before pushing past him into the room. Tom shook his head and shut the door, walking towards her as she stood with her back to him.

"Aye, come in, why don't you? I mean it's not like I live here and have any say—shit!"

He stared down at her face in horror. An angry bruise covered her right cheek, and her eye was slightly swollen. There was a cut on her lip. He tried to gently lift her chin to get a better look, and her flinch undid him. He felt a hot ball of anger against whoever had done this to her, and it took everything he had to keep himself under control. "Who did this to you?" he asked roughly.

Libby looked away, as if ashamed. That riled him even further and he knew he was on the verge of an uncontrollable red fog taking over. Tom carefully raised her chin higher, so she had no choice but to look at him. "No bull-shit, no hiding, Libby. You need to tell me who did this to you."

He thought she was going to refuse, knowing how stubborn and difficult she could be when she chose to. Yet all at once her face crumpled, and uncharacteristic defeat hung heavy in her red eyes. He had to lean close to hear her whisper, "Jake".

Tom drew sharply back, no longer trying to hide his anger. "That filthy son of a bitch!"

He pushed past her to storm towards the door, determined to find the bastard and give him a lesson he wouldn't forget. He always knew Jake had a dangerous edge to him, but at least at school there was a caring side underneath all that tough talk. The thought that someone he'd once counted as a mate could do this to Libby made Tom sick to his stomach. He grabbed the door to open it when suddenly his way was blocked. How she had moved so fast he had no idea.

"Let me get past, Lib! I won't stand for him hurting you anymore."

Instead of moving aside, she pressed closer to him, clenching hold of his t-shirt. "No! No! Shit, I don't want you to go after him, you hear me?"

Tom grabbed her hands and tried to pry them off him. But she was surprisingly strong. "I mean it, let me go! I'm going to find the bastard and make him pay."

"I said no, Tom!"

"Why the hell are you trying to stop me?" His eyes narrowed dangerously. "Are you trying to protect him? Because if you are, so help me—"

Hot angry tears erupted from her. She shouted, "I'm trying to protect you, you eejit!"

That threw him, made him pause. "I can look after myself."

Her hands were clenching his clothes so hard, Tom thought his t-shirt would tear, the same way her next words did. "He'll kill you!" There was a small dangerous pause. "And then he'll kill me."

With that, she pressed her head against his chest, shaking violently. His arms came around her as if they had no choice, while his mind whirled with the shocking reality they found themselves in.

Holy crap...

MARCUS WAS SWALLOWING HIS COFFEE, flinching as the scalding liquid hit the back of his throat, while eyeing the time. Food would have to wait, even though the smell of toast wafting from the kitchen threatened to be his undoing. They'd overslept, badly, mainly because they'd forgot to set the alarm. Too distracted last night to remember. A small, satisfied smile tugged at the corners of his mouth. He could never get enough of his wife. She made him feel alive, on fire. What she did to him...

He could hear her in the kitchen now, washing up. She looked far away, staring out of the window as he walked up behind her. Her hand was constantly washing over the same spot on the bowl.

"Ach, I think you might be rubbing the pattern away there," he commented dryly, smiling faintly. Sophia started a bit, and sud-filled water splashed up and hit him square on the trousers. He jumped back, reaching for a cloth. "Ahh, going to look like I pissed myself now."

"Don't come up behind me like that then! Trying to give me heart failure?" Sophia reached down and gave a half-hearted attempt to dry off the water, only to make it worse as the cloth was wetter than his trousers. She looked up, pulling a sorry face. "I'm not helping, am I?"

Marcus raised an eyebrow, "Not in any way. I'm going to change out of these. But listen, before I do, we have to talk about Aneella. I know, I know," he rushed on as she went to break in, "I hear your concerns and I get it; I really do." He reached out and cupped her face, searching her eyes. "But I really want to bring that bastared down for good and out of our lives, and the only way I can do that is to draw him out. She's the only one who can. I can reach a deal with her."

Sophia bit her lip—a sign of nervousness. He hadn't seen that in a long time. She'd used to do it all the time when their lives first clashed together.

"Maybe I could..."

Marcus waited a moment. "You could what?" he prompted when she stayed silent.

"Maybe I could go over to Cathy's and see how it is with Aneella."

A strange feeling stirred in him, the same feeling he got when he knew someone wasn't being honest with him. She had changed what she was going to say. But this was Sophia, and they vowed to always be honest with each other. Marcus had told her many times he found it hard to trust others.

Pushing aside these disturbing thoughts, he kissed her and said, "I would really appreciate that," before moving quickly away into the bedroom, his throat too thick to say anything else. Five minutes later and he made a swift exit, giving her a faint smile as he left.

I STOOD THERE, the dripping cloth still in my hand, and all I could think was that he knew. He knew I'd lied to him.

113

In a moment of selfish need, I had become unguarded. I couldn't let that happen again. I had to keep him in the dark, otherwise I couldn't do this without him stopping me to protect me.

But a lie was still a lie and oh god, it didn't feel good.

[18]

As soon as the door opened and I took one look at her pale, drawn face, my heart contracted with pity.

I smiled as warmly as I could and held out the sunflowers I had in my hand. Their striking brightness seemed to contrast sharply with the gloom of the day, a heavy rain mist still lingering over us.

"Hello, hope it's okay to just drop 'round like this," I said softly.

Cathy stared at me, then the flowers, and it was clear she was struggling to hold back the tears. "Oh, my dear, it's so good to see you." She pulled me into a tight hug, almost crushing the flowers between us. I held her against me, closing my eyes as I realised I needed this as much as she did.

I wasn't used to warm, motherly hugs. My mother was a very distant presence in my life: I was lucky to get an occasional phone call. Even during all those weeks recovering in hospital, she had only visited a couple of times, blaming the distance for why she couldn't come more. She had attended my first wedding only because she adored Richard

115

and was forever telling me how lucky I was to have snagged him. To this day, she still couldn't accept what he had done to me. On my wedding day to Marcus, it was all too clear she didn't want to be there, that she didn't approve of my choice of husband, or where we lived. I was immensely relieved when she left early. Marcus, who came from a big noisy clan of a family, had been utterly lost for words over her—a first for him. It seemed I hadn't been part of her plans to have a child, so most of my childhood had been spent with different childminders and family relatives who resented looking after me as much as I resented being looked after by them. I used to try and make myself invisible by curling up in a corner out of sight, pretending my home life was so very different. I'd never known my father. All I had of him was one faded, crumpled photo of a dark-haired, green-eyed man whom I took after. Mum had refused to tell me anything about him anytime I pleaded her to, but I had worked out that I must have been the result of an affair, because in the photo, he had worn a wedding band. I had tried vainly to find out who he was, but with no name on the birth certificate, it had been a fruitless, soul-destroying search. I vowed to myself there and then that my children would have a loving father in their lives.

Cathy, sweet, caring Cathy, was everything I had yearned for my own mum to be. No wonder I had been drawn to her the moment she'd visited Ella at university with a care package. She had immediately seen the lost girl in me. When she visited next, she'd brought two care packages: one for each of us. Ella, used to a mother's love, had barely said thanks before chucking it to the side, whereas I, desperately trying not to cry, had hugged Cathy so hard that we had nearly toppled onto the bed. Cathy laughed, patting my cheek, but I could see she was touched by my reaction. Though we'd lost touch after Ella cut me out of her life and I married Richard, I never forgot her kindness.

Now it was my turn to look after her, this beautiful woman who had given me love when I needed it.

"I'm so sorry," I quietly murmured against her as we held tight.

I felt a sob shudder against my shoulder before she reluctantly drew back. She gave me a watery smile, touching my cheek. "What a state we're in," she said with a shaky laugh. "And these poor, beautiful sunflowers getting squashed like this. Dear me."

I smiled, "Why don't we find some water for them, to revive them? If it's okay for me to come in?"

"Oh of course, of course, where are my manners?" Cathy shook her head as she urged me in. I found my eyes drifting towards the lounge as we walked down the hall-way, almost expecting to see Derek lying there. Instead, I was confronted with the stark reality of an empty, cold bed with idle medical equipment. Even his spirit no longer lingered.

Shaking off an eerie realisation of my own mortality, I quickly followed Cathy into her kitchen. She stood in the middle, looking a little confused as to what she was meant to be doing. My heart lurched for her.

"Where do you keep your vase?" I prompted.

"Oh yes... yes, it's over here, dear." She walked out of the kitchen into what was Derek's bedroom and came back in with a chipped blue vase, filled with flowers now dry and drooping. Cathy stilled as she held it in front of her. "Derek brought this for me on our first wedding anniver-sary. We were saving so hard for our first house; you see, we wanted to start a family." She gave a short laugh, "Derek said this would be the first thing we would put in the house and that we would always fill it with flowers."

She turned to me then, eyes wet with tears. "He kept his promise too, every week buying me flowers... that was, until he couldn't anymore. Then I kept the vase filled for him. I think he was able to smell them there." Cathy was looking intently at me as if seeking confirmation.

I found myself nodding, fighting back my own emotions. "I'm sure he did, and it brought him joy."

She gave me a grateful smile. "Thank you. Thank you, Sophia."

"Would you like me to arrange them for you?" I indicated towards the vase.

"Oh, why yes, my dear, please."

As I set to work on arranging the flowers after throwing away the old ones, it was like something had been released in Cathy. She began to reminisce about her early days with Derek. The now boiled kettle was forgotten. I was given a glimpse into the life of a man I had never known. A man it turned out I wished I had known, to have felt his gentle, caring ways and quiet manners, working hard to provide for his wife and daughter. Ella had never really spoken about him, in the way that someone secure in her father's love didn't need to.

"He always loved his fish supper on a Sunday, I never could change him on that! Ella always used to beg us to have something different, but even she couldn't persuade him, even though she was the apple of his eye."

"He really must have loved his fish," I laughed, "knowing how persuasive Ella can be!"

Cathy smiled as she sat down opposite me, smiling wistfully. "That she is, my girl. I often wonder what our other younger darling girl would have been like, had she lived."

I whipped my head up the flowers. *Had I heard her right?* "Your... other girl?"

"Yes, Amy. We lost her when she was nine."

I stared at her, my mind whirling with what she said so matter-of-factly. *How much suffering can one person take, and stay standing?*

"I'm so sorry," I whispered. "I had no idea. Ella never mentioned Amy..."

Cathy shook her head, patting my hand. "How could you know?" She hesitated. "Ella blamed herself, you see. She was walking Amy to school when she saw some friends and ran on ahead. Amy went to run to catch up and she didn't ... she never saw the car coming too fast around the bend." Cathy looked down, swallowing. This time it was me squeezing her hand. She squeezed back. "It was just an unfortunate accident, but something changed in my fun-loving daughter the day we lost her sister. So, when Derek had his stroke, Ella became obsessed with finding a way to save him and bring him back to us. I never could convince her that there was nothing we could do. I could never manage to get her to let go of her guilt."

Her voice trailed away, and I sat there, stunned. It was like everything I thought I had known about Aneella was suddenly blurred out and in came this sharper, clearer image of a troubled, guilt-ridden woman concealed behind a selfish, ambitious facade. How could I merge the two together to even comprehend who Aneella really was?

After a moment of silence, Cathy grew suddenly agitated, grasping my hand so tight I bit my lip. "Ella must come to Derek's funeral, she must! She'll never accept he's gone otherwise. Please, can your husband help me? The prison won't tell me anything, I don't even know if she's been granted special compassionate leave, and she won't let me visit her. Sophia, I don't know what else to do."

She broke down then, and I pulled her close, closing my eyes against the waves of gasping pain. Everything in me rebelled against using Aneella to draw out Richard. Yet still I must find a way to persuade her to come to her father's funeral, and that meant we had to do it Marcus' way.

"I'll do everything I can," I promised, stroking her back.

"Thank you, thank you, dear."

We held each other for a moment, then she drew back. There was a fierceness in her eyes as she held my face between her hands, ensuring my eyes were captured by hers.

"Promise me, Sophia, that you'll never stop fighting for those you love. We can live without a lot in our lives. But not love, never love. Without it, our hearts will shrivel up and die. So, fight for those you love, with every breath you have."

[19]

Hamish, still officially a Glasgow PC by day, but moonlighting to earn extra money with nighttime surveillance, was dozing in an unmarked blue car... until there was a loud knock on the passenger window. He jolted, looking bewilderedly around him. Jerry was standing there, mouthing at him through the glass, holding two coffees and bacon rolls. Vigorously rubbing his face, Hamish opened the passenger door.

Jerry climbed into the seat, handing one of the coffees and rolls to him, while muttering "What the hell were you doing sleeping on the job?"

"Sorry," Hamish muttered as he took a grateful bite of the bacon roll, tomato sauce oozing out as he did.

"You're a lucky wee lad I'm not the kind who tells on you though God knows how I landed this babysitting role. Thought I was done with night-time surveillance, freezing my balls off. Hate Glasgow—Oi!" Jerry protested, as Hamish frantically began to wave his hands around, spilling hot coffee over them both. "What the—"

"Look!" Hamish pointed towards the front door, swallowing so hard on his mouthful that he nearly went into a full-scale coughing fit.

Jerry followed Hamish's finger. When he saw what had got Hamish so excited, he immediately reached for his phone.

After a couple of rings, the phone was answered. "Sir? We've got action," Jerry exclaimed.

THE NEXT DAY, Marcus was anxiously awaiting the return of his sergeant, Jerry. Unable to sit still, he had been constantly asking Tom if he'd heard from Jerry. Each time, with the impatience all twenty-somethings exhibited so brilliantly, especially while working on another job their boss had set, Tom would roll his eyes and give a pointed shake of his head. After the sixth rolling of eyes, Marcus realised he may be pushing his luck and bid a quick retreat, turning his attention to what they uncovered about *Slyfox*.

What they knew so far was that Slyfox was most certainly the name given to this operation, created by Richard. Tom was investigating the phone number. They wouldn't have long before this number was no longer active, as was the way with burner phones. Yet one huge step forward had been made. As Marcus had suspected, the texts had predominantly been sent from the Glasgow location, which is why he had sent Jerry to run the surveillance operation. And was why he was now itching for Jerry to get here with whatever photo ID they had as to who had been seen entering the flat. Marcus was not going to trust anyone else, including the Glasgow officers, who would have no qualms about hustling in and taking over.

Sophia had been visibly upset when she got back from seeing Cathy. Something that was becoming a little too frequent of late and which he did not enjoy seeing. She had told him what had happened, how desperate Cathy was to see her daughter. To his utter surprise she had urged him to do whatever it took to get Aneella to attend the funeral.

"You understand that means we'll ask her to be taped up and make contact with Richard, aye?" He had carefully asked.

Sophia had slowly nodded, "I know." She paused. "I want to come with you when you see Aneella and also come to the funeral."

Marcus shook his head vehemently. "No, no way, I'm not letting you anywhere loose with the possibility of Richard and god knows who in the vicinity."

Sophia had come up close and put her hands on his chest. "I'm not worried."

"I am!"

"This isn't about me. It's about Cathy, and Ella, saying goodbye to Derek. I won't let them down, especially not Cathy. She has no one, Marcus! And if it means we bring Richard and whoever he's working with out in the open because of it, then all the better." Marcus went to interject. She covered his mouth with her fingers. "You're not going to change my mind. End of." Sophia then removed her fingers and kissed him, smiling confidently.

Yet he swore he felt a tremor go through her body.

MARCUS WAS JUST GETTING off the phone to book a visit to Inverness Prison the next day when Jerry came flying in, looking flushed and quite animated.

"Sorry, sir, I got here as fast as I could!"

Marcus grinned. "As long as you didn't speed."

"Aye, well I may have put the blue light on driving the A9 to get round those *bampot* tourists."

Marcus laughed. "Careful. We need those 'idiot' tourists

to keep this country afloat. I'll get you a coffee, then you can fill me in."

Jerry's eyes widened. "You don't need to do that-"

"For having to not only do a night shift but get yourself back here in under two and a half hours, ach, it's the least I can do."

HALF AN HOUR LATER, spread out before them were photos Jerry and Hamish had captured of two men entering the flat.

"How long were they in the premises?" Marcus asked, as he stared hard at the photo with the clearest image. One of the men, unshaven with coppery brown, shaggy hair, was looking in their direction, almost as if he had sensed he was being watched. The other man, who was shorter in stature and had a blue baseball cap hung low over his head, was turned away, making him harder to identify. However, his coat seemed of an expensive cut compared to the others, and Marcus's instincts told him this man could be heading it up. Perhaps he was the one Richard had seemed so afraid of all those months ago at their confrontation, when Sophia was stabbed.

"No more than forty-five minutes, tops. Then they left together and got into a red sedan."

"Got the number plate?"

There was a brief silence, making Marcus finally look up from staring at the photo. Marcus smiling faintly at Jerry's indignant face. "I'll take that as an aye, then."

"You do that, sir. You do that."

Marcus pointed at the copper-haired man. "Let's get a positive identity on this guy asap. Get all the departments and Glasgow onto it. Have Tom help you. But not tonight, tomorrow morning," he added as Jerry went to stand up. "It's late and you've had a long shift. I don't want you burning out on me, aye? I'm going to see Ms. Blair in the morning at the prison, and I'm taking Sophia with me."

Jerry raised his eyebrows in surprise. "Has Ms. Blair agreed to be taped?"

Marcus gave a wiry smile. "Not yet."

"Ah, I see," Jerry nodded. "Using your secret weapon in the hope to persuade. Good luck, sir."

"Thanks," Marcus pulled a face. "Think we're going to need it."

Jerry gave a gruff laugh as he walked out of the room.

FEELING the need to let off some pent-up emotion, I headed to our garage to practise on the punch bag Marcus had put up for me. It had quickly become my own form of therapy, releasing some much-needed endorphins and biting frustration. I was still hoping that somehow if we could bring Richard out into the open at the funeral, I wouldn't have to meet him alone,

As the sweat left a trail down my spine, I was vaguely aware of a door slamming somewhere. My lungs screaming in protest, I kept going for another ten minutes before his voice disrupted me.

"Looking *mhath*, Mrs. Armstrong. And hot," Marcus added with a wink, running an eye over my leggings and workout bra.

I leaned over, trying to catch my breath, unable to answer him, then managed to get out, "*Mhath?*" My eyes narrowed at him. Marcus put up his hands in defence.

"Means 'good'. It's a compliment, I swear!"

I gave him as stern a look as I could muster with sweat pouring off my forehead. From his amused look, my sternness was not having an effect. "Hmmm. Well, hot is right, a hot, sweaty mess. Lord save me..." I groaned.

Marcus laughed. "Aye, maybe that too. But they say sweat is weakness leaving your body."

"Do they indeed?" I muttered as I tried to undo my boxing gloves, which was harder to do than it sounded. Seeing my struggle, Marcus stepped over and deftly freed me from them, then snuck in a kiss.

"You're brave," I laughed.

"I like my woman hot and sweaty," he murmured, pulling me close to him, drawing me into another kiss. A few moments later, when we finally pulled apart, a sudden thought came to me.

"What were you doing inside before you came here?"

Marcus gave me a confused look. "I haven't been in the house yet. I parked up and saw you in here. Why?"

I shook my head. "I thought I heard a door slam inside the house a few minutes ago. But I must have been mistaken. Unless the wind caused it to bang."

"Maybe I should go check." His face had gone from confused to a deep frown within a microsecond. I reached out to stop him as he made to leave.

"I'm sure it's all fine, Mr. Detective. And anyway, more importantly, you haven't told me if you're seeing Aneella tomorrow or not."

That made him pause, stare down at me. I found myself holding my breath in anticipation. "Aye, aye, I am... and much to my reluctance, you're coming with me."

[20]

Across the other side of the city, the full moon cast an eerie glow over Inverness River, the water still and flat beneath it.

Tom stared out at the moonlight from the top floor window of his bedroom yet found no comfort from the foreboding thoughts scattering and darkening his mind. A hot, dangerous anger burned through his veins, and it was taking everything not to go find Jake and kick the living shit out of him. Even now, his hands were clenching and unclenching into fists by his side.

It was only two things that stopped him, and even then, this thin resistance could snap all too easily.

The first was that he had sworn an oath to uphold the law when he joined the police force. Beating up a man, even with very good reasons—and seeing a battered woman more than qualified —would result in being kicked off the force, no question. That was an oath he couldn't break.

The second was sleeping in his bed, curled up in a tight ball next to him. Tom turned and looked at her. The moonlight cast a shadow over the contours of her face, making the large bruise seem even more horrific. She looked much younger than her twenty-three years lying there, with her thin body showing the outline of her bones. A gripping wave of panic washed over him, overwhelming him with the enormity of being responsible for her and everything she brought. He wasn't cut out for this. How the hell was he meant to help her? Protect her? He could barely look after himself.

Yet what else could he do except keep her here with him, while they tried to figure a way out of this situation? No way was he letting her back on the streets so that bastard could hurt her again.

Now all he needed to do was think.

And keep them alive.

Then keep her out of prison.

As well as control his temper.

So, nothing much then...

THE MOONLIGHT HAD GIVEN way to a striking sunrise that seemed to cover the whole expanse of the sky in glorious splendour. The vibrant red to burnt orange hues, that blended into golden yellow, rose from behind the distant Munro Mountain and lit the loch into moving fire, flames dancing over the surface.

Marcus leaned against the wooden frame of the veranda, the coffee in his hand forgotten as he drank in the view, appreciating mother earth putting on a breathtaking show. Mornings like this were a precious rarity and stirred his soul and his love for this country he had been privileged to be born into. There was nowhere else he wanted to live but right here on his own piece of Scottish Highlands, where the glen was fresh and rich, and the air was alive with the sound of buzzards calling to each other as they soared above the tree canopy.

"There you are. Do we need to go?"

Hearing her voice, he turned and smiled at her, then reached out to take her hand to pull her to him. Positioning Sophia in front of him so she was leaning against his chest, he bent to murmur in her ear, stirring the tendrils of her hair as he did. "Take a moment, *mo leannan*. Look what bonnie delight mother nature has brought for us today."

He felt her soften and lean back against him as she gazed at the sunrise. He knew she was smiling, before she mumbled, "Every sunrise we're given..."

Marcus smiled, pressing his lips against her hair as he finished, "We don't waste a single moment that follows. And we won't, I promise."

They stood there, arms tight around each other, letting the aura of the sunrise as it rose high in the sky to soothe their troubled minds.

AN HOUR LATER, and already the promise of the sunrise had faded to overcast grey clouds laden with the threat of rain. But I clung to the memory of its rich, vibrant colours as I once again stepped into the cold, insipid walls of Inverness Prison. This time, instead of a smaller, separate room, we were shown into a larger room filled with a few plastic chairs paired off with a chipped table wedged between them. Over by the wall, opposite to where we now sat, was a drinks machine with a handwritten note stuck above with peeling sellotape asking for a 20p donation for tea/coffee. In the corner was a box filled with children's toys, some worn and tatty and looking as sad as I felt thinking about those innocent hands who'd played with them. I dragged my eyes away, closing them for a moment.

"You okay?"

I turned and nodded at Marcus. "I just want to get this over with. This place makes me feel uncomfortable."

"Aye, aye, me too. Hopefully Aneella will be in a co-operative mood."

I raised my eyebrows, and Marcus gave a short, humourless laugh.

"Maybe a little optimistic, ach?"

I was about to reply when a prison officer appeared at the door. I craned my neck to look behind her, unconsciously sucking my breath in, aware that Marcus grew still by my side. They walked towards us, the officer blocking my view of Aneella following behind with another prison officer. It seemed a frustrating eternity before I finally locked eyes with her.

When I did, I wish I hadn't.

MARCUS SENSED Sophia draw back into her chair, as if trying to put space between her and Aneella. They were trapped in an eye-lock that seemed to be taking all the resentful fire burning darkly in Aneella's eyes into Sophia's startled ones. He had never seen this heat in Aneella before, this blinding anger. Usually there was a cunning, almost closed-off look about her as she played her games with them. This was something altogether new and seemed to be directed solely at Sophia. She had become unpredictable... and that made her dangerous. He felt the stir of nervousness in his stomach and knew he had made a fatal mistake in bringing Sophia. All he could do now was try and salvage the situation.

"Ms. Blair, we appreciate you agreeing to see us today."

"You speak as if I had a choice in it," came the tart reply, as if dismissing him. With her eyes still fixed on

Sophia, Aneella leaned forward in the chair, her body buzzing. In contrast, Sophia had grown very, very still.

"You were meant to come straight to me as soon as you heard." Leaning closer again, enforcing Sophia to see everything spitting out from within her. "You should have got here first."

There was a brief tense silence, the air static as if holding its breath.

Then Marcus, frowning hard, said "What do you mean, first? Has someone already visited you?"

"Now, wouldn't you like to know."

ANEELLA LIKED the feel of this simmering anger coursing through her veins, turning her blood into molten lava. It felt good, so damn good. It had been too long since she had allowed it to rise to the surface and take control. At least the constant fear of what was going to happen to her was diminished, and the grief that threatened to tear her apart inside was momentarily smothered.

She knew why they were here, thinking she was ripe to be used for their doing. They were fools if they thought she would be played by them, go along without a fight. She would make Sophia pay for not coming immediately, for withdrawing from her.

No one walked away from her.

UNLIKE MARCUS, I had seen this rage inside Aneella before. It had begun the day Richard had shown interest in me at the bar, and flashes of it would come back whenever I questioned her actions. A vivid memory came storming back of one day near the end of our time at university. I had been on the phone to an annoyed Richard, grovelling, apologising for being late, as I always seemed to be. This time it was because my professor had held me back. Richard cut off our call. My stomach twisted.

The door opposite to where I stood opened. I looked up from my phone. Aneella and her professor were standing in the doorway, bodies pressed close together. I found myself staring, wide eyed, as she reached up and gave the professor a lingering kiss on the mouth, then turned and stepped out into the hallway. The professor quickly shut the door behind her, not noticing me.

I was toying with the cowardly instinct to bolt before I was seen when I heard her say my name. *Crap.* My feet seemed to be rooted to the spot as she took slow, deliberate steps towards me. If there was a brief glimpse of panic in her blue eyes, it was quickly smothered, replaced with a hot spark as she faced me head-on.

"What are you doing here?"

I swallowed. "My professor wanted to see me... as it seemed yours did too."

Aneella remained silent, still staring hard at me. Then she gave a nonchalant shrug, caring little, it seemed, about what I thought, before turning from me and walking down the corridor.

Despite her determination to cut me off, expecting me to keep my mouth shut, I found myself nonetheless doing something out of character—I ran up and grabbed her arm.

"Ella, please be careful! He's known for being a leech. I don't want you to get hurt—"

Aneella abruptly stopped and jerked my hand off. This time I was met with the full force of her rage as she hissed. "Don't ever touch me like that again. Has it occurred to you that I'm using him?"

"Using him? For what?" I gasped.

Aneella gave me a long knowing, taunting look,

eyebrows raised. I began to feel sick as I realised what she insinuated.

"Oh... I see. Couldn't be bothered to study?"

Aneella stepped right up to me, taking my chin in her hand, squeezing it so painfully I had to bite back a cry.

"Didn't I tell you I always get what I want?"

I let her get away with it, pretend I hadn't seen or known anything. In other words, I became the timid coward expected of me. Last year, I found out from her other professor, Anthony, that she not only 'got help' on coursework but cheated on her final exams.

I'd be a total liar if I said it hadn't crossed my mind now, in this prison, to retreat far away from her anger.

But then Cathy's grief-stricken face came into my mind and a new steely determination rose within me.

I leaned forward, crossing my arms and meeting her with an equal fire burning in my eyes. "Cut the crap, Ella, and start making this right. Your mum is hurting badly. You are refusing to come to the funeral even though Marcus and the prison can arrange it for you. You have to do whatever it takes to get to it—your dad deserves nothing less from you."

MARCUS LOOKED at his wife and tried to hide his smile of relief and his appreciation. There was that inner fighting spirit he'd missed over the last few months. Sophia had begun to show it, then life had crushed it when it was still new and vulnerable. Now she was fighting back against this bully. For that was exactly what Aneella was—a clever, manipulative bully who had had everything her way up to now, even while in here. No more.

He too leaned forward, unconsciously symmetrical to his wife. "You can do this the hard way, Ms. Blair, or the easy way. But only with the easy way, where you co-operate with us, will you gain favour in your trial." He paused to let his words sink in. "But be assured of one thing - you will attend this funeral."

Aneella sat back, crossing her arms, her mask falling back over her face until it become bland and unreadable. "I'm listening," She gave a mocking smile. "Do tell me how the easy way benefits me."

Marcus and I both glanced at each other, surprised. Why had she yielded so suddenly? And where was all that rage from a few minutes ago? It occurred to me then – Aneella was the epitome of Jekyll and Hyde, slipping in and out of both, and neither side of her was truly safe to be around.

My husband gave a small shrug, as if to say, *let's go with this*. I gave a small nod.

Marcus leaned forward. "A good choice. It's fairly straightforward. What we will need from you is to simply wear a wire on the day of your father's funeral."

"A simple wire ... interesting. Why would you need me to do that?"

Marcus hesitated before replying with, "With the recent activity we have interpreted and your previous assistance we are aware that your—as yet unidentified—former associates are keeping close tabs on you. We believe they will be somewhere watching the funeral. They may try to contact you."

Aneella's eyes narrowed. "So, you want me to be your bait."

"Aye, in a manner of speaking. We will be giving you a taped phone and will leak this number out anonymously to cover all possible means of communication."

Her eyes widened. "And while I'm luring them out in the open for you, while of course trying to mourn the loss of my dad, do tell me: how the hell you plan to keep me safe?" As she said this in a mocking tone, her eyes swung to me, as if directing the question at me. As I opened my mouth to say... well, I'm not sure what, Marcus thankfully cut in.

"My officers will be there in plain clothes, and I can assure you, your safety is of the utmost priority at all times."

Aneella shook her head, giving a scoffing laugh. "You can assure my safety." She suddenly leaned across the table. "Do you have any idea how dangerous these bastards can be? As far as they're concerned, I've betrayed them, and trust me, they don't take kindly to that kind of shit."

If I hadn't been staring so intentionally, I might have missed it. I saw the briefest flicker of fear darken her irises, and beads of sweat break out on her forehead before both were wiped away. It was enough to awaken the tiniest flicker of the once all-consuming love I had for her. I reached out to grab her hand.

Aneella stilled, looking down at my hand on hers before lifting her head to me. "You can trust him to keep you safe, I swear to you," I urged. "He *will* protect you."

There was a moment of utter silence, where only our breathing could be heard.

"Fine. I'll do it."

Marcus and I broke out in a relieved smile.

"You've made a good decision, Ms. Blair, and I'll make sure the judge who will be conducting your trail knows of your co-operation." Marcus nodded.

"He's right, you're helping yourself. And you'll be there for your mum. I'll be there too," I reassured, helping to coax a reaction from her stony face. I could feel Marcus' hard stare on me as I said those last words. I shot him a look to say, *Don't argue with me now!* Fortunately, one thing

Marcus was good at was picking up on signals. He turned back to Aneella.

"Your father's funeral is in three days. I will visit you here first thing with my sergeant and we'll wire you up. Then I will have my officers escort you over. Does that all make sense?"

Aneella shrugged, "Fine." She stood. The two prison officers who had been discreetly in the background immediately stepped forward on either side of her. We also stood.

Aneella turned to leave, and I was glad. Suddenly I wanted out of here, badly. But she'd barely taken one step when she paused, turned back.

Her eyes, those hard glittery eyes that could mercilessly burn a hole straight into your soul, bored into me as she uttered, "But remember this, if anything happens to me, it will be on you." She leaned closer, her warm breath scolding my skin. "And that guilt knowing you were the reason I was harmed... it will break you, my darling Sophia. It will break you apart."

[21]

He stared at his phone like an addict fixated on his next hit. He'd lost count of the number of times he'd refreshed his email to see if there was a reply or had a missed call from her. Each time, nothing. Bloody nothing.

He swore as he stepped out into the biting cold of the Yorkshire Dales. He was scared, so shit-scared. They were losing patience and had given him an ultimatum, one he didn't much like. He didn't care what happened to her, she was already done for. But he wasn't going down without a fight or ending up dead at the bottom of a lake.

His phone began vibrating in his hand and his stomach lurched. For a moment he dared to believe it was finally her. Then he looked at the caller ID and he squeezed his eyes shut as his heart clenched in gripping apprehension, even as he reluctantly pressed Accept.

MARCUS STEPPED onto the veranda with two steaming cups of coffee, where Sophia was curled up on the bench with her favourite tartan blanket tucked around her. He smiled down at her as she accepted one of the mugs. "Here, this'll warm your cockles. I've added a wee drop of whisky. We deserve it after today, that we do."

Sophia shook her head, finally smiling. She had hardly said anything since leaving the prison, despite his best efforts to reassure her that Aneella would be kept safe, and that they were merely playing mind games with her. "You know I'm a gin girl all the way, no matter how often you try and slip that whisky into my drink."

Marcus gave a theatrical gasp, grabbing his chest. "Ach, you cut my heart and make it bleed with such blasphemy of my native nectar of the gods. Tsh, that would have been a hanging crime up here in the Highlands a few centuries back."

Sophia merely raised her eyebrows, unmoved. "Centuries back, there's no way I would have been welcomed, nor, for that matter, would I have wanted to come to this heathen land, to be able to refuse your so-called nectar of the gods."

He laughed, settling down next to her. "Aye, true, true. You would have been chased out of this wilderness and back over Hadrian's wall, where you belonged."

"You think I'd have wanted to live with all those blood-thirsty, axe-wielding Highlanders? Uhhh, no."

He grinned, "I would have enjoyed it, dressed in my clan tartan, warrior paint slashed across my cheeks as I roared into battle with only my axe to protect my crown jewels."

Sophia snorted.

Keeping his voice casual, Marcus continued. "And talking of tartan and kilts and all things Scottish, fancy going to your first ceilidh tonight?"

She turned and stared at him. "Huh?"

"A ceilidh, you know, our traditional dance, taught to us

when we were but wee nippers of sixteen. It's merely there to endure the excruciating moment of asking some wee girl to take pity and dance with us."

Sophia was trying not to laugh. "And did you get some kind-hearted girl to take pity and dance with you, or were you left standing by the wall?"

Marcus raised his eyebrows in what he hoped was a confident way. "How could you doubt my charming ways, lass?"

"So that was a negative on the girl then..."

He shook his head sadly, giving her his most sorrowful look. "That wall was a lonely, cruel place to be when you're a wee, shy, spotty teenager."

It worked like a dream. Sophia reached across and kissed him soothingly, snuggling closer. "Their loss, my gain," she murmured.

Marcus made the most of kissing her before pulling back to push his advantage. "So, you see I need you to put my 'standing by a cold wall' ghosts to rest by coming and dancing with me. There's one happening in Inverness tonight. Jerry told me about it. Aye, apparently, he's a bit of a closet dancer. Who knew."

"But don't you usually only have those around Hogmanay, or... or weddings or something?"

He gave her a pointed look. "We're Scottish. Do we ever need a reason to have a dram and knees up?"

She still wasn't looking totally convinced. "Apart from that one time by the loch when you tried to teach me—"

"Aye, when you decided to test my lifesaving skills." *Would he ever forget that?*

Sophia pulled a face. "No need for the reminder. Anyway, having no other training in this I'm not sure I'm ready for a public ceilidh."

"Ach, it's easy." He grinned. "You'll be grand. Just follow

139

my lead. Not one for normally saying no to a challenge..." He reached down and cupped her cheek so that she was looking at him. "It'll be good to go out, have some fun. It's been a tough couple of weeks. We need this, *mo leannan.*"

He found himself holding his breath, desperately wanting her to say yes. They needed this night, for them, for their still-young marriage, to have a much-needed change of scene from here, where something was putting him on edge. More than once, he had had the eerie sense they were being watched. Every acute sense within him was telling him something dangerous was coming their way, and that they needed to be strong, united. He was just praying their love could withhold anything thrown at them.

Sophia gave a small, resigned sigh. "Fine, fine, for you and your sixteen-year-old spotty wallflower self, I'll go. But don't blame me if I injure your toes from stamping on them."

"Ach, no problem, I've got steel-capped boots for such an occasion."

JERRY WAS PACKING UP, more than ready to finish for the day at the station. He was thinking about how soon he could get over to the ceilidh and join Marcus and Sophia. His face always hid a thousand emotions. He'd learned to his cost to always keep a bland, neutral expression. Internally, now that was a different story—he was bouncing with excitement and raring to get there. It wasn't something he told many people; his love for ceilidh dancing, and his ex-wife certainly never understood his enthusiasm for it. But then she never really got him, full stop, so no surprise there. He rarely allowed himself a chance to let go, to truly release himself from the restraints he put onto himself, like a belt that only tightened, never slackened... except for when it came to ceilidhs.

He hadn't planned to invite Marcus and Sophia, truth be told. But Marcus had come back from visiting Ms. Blair troubled, deeply troubled, concerned for his wife and this never-ending strain on their marriage. On impulse, Jerry had said that what they needed was a fun night out. Marcus had given a sorrowful laugh, saying, any ideas? And before he knew it, he was inviting his boss along. Now, with Marcus texting saying that they were coming, he felt he'd done something good and that made him exceptionally happy. He held a deep respect for Marcus, someone who had come under a lot of flak from other DIs who resented him rising to this position so quickly, yet had proven each one of them wrong, even with his marriage to Sophia, a former suspect. That's why he was as determined as his boss to finally bring this case to court and break the fraud ring, along with getting justice for Sophia who'd been attacked not once, but twice now.

As he turned off the light on his desk, Jerry looked across to see Tom sitting immobile in front of his computer, staring at the screen.

"Tom?" No reply, Tom didn't even move. Jerry frowned, stepping closer. "Tom, you alright there?"

Perhaps sensing him close, Tom gave a start and turned to stare at Jerry without really seeing him. Seeing Jerry's eyes flick across to the screen—open on a case file of a photo of a young woman he didn't recognise—Tom quickly minimised the screen. He gave Jerry a smile that didn't reach his eyes and didn't fool either of them.

"New case you're working on?" Jerry casually asked.

There was a glimpse of panic in Tom's eyes, before he turned away, concentrating very hard on the screen in front of him as he rushed out, "No, no, I was searching for any names that contained fox and that one appeared... but I don't think it's relevant. Off home?"

"Aye, I am. You should too. It's late. Don't burn yourself out," Jerry replied, concern edging his voice.

Tom finally turned to look at him, gave him a more natural smile. "Yeah, I will. I'm a little beat. Have a good night."

Jerry gave a nod, paused, debated saying something more, but in the end only said, "See you in the morning," before grabbing his coat to leave.

Something made him turn and look back when he got to the door. Tom was sitting forward now, his hands cradling his bowed head.

TOM LOOKED up to see the retreating back of Jerry, and shame washed over him. He wasn't used to that damning feeling. Up till now, he'd lived a carefree existence, where life had been free of consequences and given him permission to be a bit of an obnoxious, smug asshole.

But was he behaving any better now?

Could he justify what he was about to do as morally right, when everything screamed at him that it was wrong, that not only would this cost him his job, but have him face possible criminal charges? Did it matter that he was doing it to try and save her? Would anyone give a damn about that? Did she?

He clicked on the screen he'd concealed from Jerry—the open file on Jake. Once more, she stared out at him, despite the graininess of the photo. Tom felt a weird shudder go through him as he hovered the mouse over the delete button for her photo, the cursor blinking furiously at him. Her pale, pleading voice came back to him from this morning as she went onto her knees to him. "You've gotta do this for me! Make my photo disappear. I can't do time for that bastard. You care about me, right?"

Tom swore, trying to rub away the brewing headache that was gathering like a storm behind his eyes. Just like then, he felt paralysed. He could still feel her small hands reaching out to pull him down to her, pressing her slim body in close to him, immediately stirring him as she began to press kisses on his face and neck in an urgent manner. Everything in him wanted to take her right then, cover her mouth with his, rip off the t-shirt that barely covered her, and finally touch every part of her like he'd been fantasising about. He was only human, damn it, and she was hot, so goddamn hot. But even as he began to kiss her, groaning a little, something made him look into her eyes. They were wide and not flickered with desire like his was, but they held an urgency, bordering on fear. She didn't kiss him because she wanted him like he did her. She was doing it to make him do exactly what she wanted.

Tom immediately yanked back like he had been burnt by a hot rod, shaking his head as he shook away her hand and backed off the bed. "No, no... don't you dare do that."

She stared up at him in that same desperate way he would see in his nightmares later.

"Tom?"

Tom felt the sudden humiliating feeling of wanting to cry, which made his voice rougher and angrier. "Don't have sex with me to get what you want. Shit, what kind of man do you take me for? You think that's the only way you'll get me to help you? Don't compare me to that bastard who's screwed you over! I- I need to get out of here. Away from you..."

Tom ran his fingers through his hair agitatedly, then turned and stumbled to the door, raw and hurting. She came running after him and grabbed his arm.

"I'm sorry, okay! I'm sorry!" Libby dragged him around to her, trying to make him look at her. He tried not to notice the tears casting a wet trail over her angry bruise. "I know you're different, I do. But I'm shit-scared, and I don't know what to do. You're the only one I trust, the only one." Her shaking hand came up and touched his cheek, making him jolt. "You've got to help me, please! Make all of this disappear."

His skin burned at the back of his neck as if eyes were on him, even though he knew he was the last one left in the office. His conscience continued to scream in his ear as the ticking clock above him grew louder by the second.

It was just one easy click. One click, that was all.

So why was it so damn hard to do it?

Tom swore aloud once more, then again and again with growing agitation, his young mind in turmoil. It was an impossible choice. Whatever he chose, someone was going to get hurt ... or worse.

But he had to make that choice, right now.

To click. Or not.

[22]

There was a lively party atmosphere that was both intoxicating and contagious as we walked into the crowded upstairs room of the pub in the heart of Inverness. Plenty of whisky and beer was already flowing and the folk band was in full swing, enticing those there to get up and fling themselves heartily into the ceilidh dancing. Raucous laughter bellowed up to the ceiling, almost deafening in its volume.

I found myself grinning as I took it all in. Marcus held my hand tightly so as not to lose me in the fray, looking relaxed and quite a bit excited as we made our way to the bar, looking for Jerry. Spotting us first, Jerry waved his hand holding a beer, almost spilling the contents everywhere. When we got to him, he clapped Marcus on the back with a grin, then kissed me on the cheek, taking us both by surprise at this unusual display of affection. Marcus and I exchanged bemused looks. I tried not to stare at the traditional Scottish kilt and sporran Jerry was wearing, happily showing me his knobbly knees. He looked good ... but nothing compared to the man on the other side of me looking pretty darn magnificent in his own kilt. I was already having rather enjoyable thoughts as to what I'd like to do with Marcus wearing that kilt... and nothing else, especially knowing what they wore, or more precisely didn't wear, under there. Meanwhile, I'd opted for a red skater dress and boots, but was beginning to wish I had my own tartan skirt to wear as I gazed around me with admiration at the incredible display of clan colours and traditional wear on display. This country was steeped in proud traditions like I'd never come across before.

"You made it!" Jerry had to shout to be heard. Was it me, or did his voice hold a stronger Scottish twang than normal? "Here, let me buy you both a drink, aye. What can I be getting you?"

"Ach, now, let me buy you one," Marcus was insisting. Hold on, had he just become a tad thicker accented too? I bit back a laugh. Clearly, the Celtic blood in them was coming out in force tonight. No doubt after a couple of drinks it would become even stronger and harder to interpret what they were saying. *Maybe I should record them,* I thought with a cheeky smile as they leaned on the bar to be noticed by the friendly, busy barpeople attempting to keep up with the steady demand.

We somehow managed to find a table to sit at, though I had the feeling it wouldn't be for long by the way their feet were tapping on the floor in time to the beat. I had to confess, mine were tempted to do the same. I had always avoided the dance floor, feeling silly and a bit like an elephant in heels when I had been drunk enough to try once. I had ended up falling onto my arse, pulling down two rather annoyed dancers with me and being the laughingstock of our dorm for a very long and painful time... hence not stepping foot on the floor since. Until tonight. Maybe this would be my moment to lay those ghosts to rest. I'd loved dancing with Marcus at our loch. I trusted him not to let me make a complete and utter prat of myself.

Sure enough, I'd barely had two sips of my gin and lemonade when I found myself being dragged to my feet by my enthusiastic partner. It was hard to resist him tonight. His job and all that we've been facing had added strain to his face of late, an ever-present tension to his shoulders and constant concern clouding his eyes. But not tonight. Tonight, I had a laughing Marcus with a wide, mischievous grin determined to teach me how to dance. So, I let him sweep me up and onto the dance floor and allow our troubles to melt away.

The beat of the drum.

The pace of the fiddle.

The encouraging shouts from the caller.

The ancient rhythm stamping the ground beneath us, passed down from one clan to the next. A dance rich in history with its own heartbeat that no one had been able to destroy. The air flowing with us as we moved back and forth, our arms linking with strangers who were now our friends.

It was intoxicating. It was moving. It was powerful.

For the first time, I felt accepted by these proud people, no longer a stranger looking in, an outsider who had stolen one of their own. I was a part of their heart; their community and I were humbled by it. As we took a break for a much-needed drink, and were immediately surrounded by locals laughing and joking with us as we raised a loud 'slainte' with our drinks, I felt such a giddy happiness come over me.

The evening seemed to fly by, and the hour was getting late, if I was reading my watch correctly in the poor lighting. But no one seemed inclined to be slowing down anytime soon. I found myself being spun around by a grinning, toothless gentleman with ruddy cheeks and a twinkle in his eyes. He was trying to say something to me, and I couldn't understand one single word. Laughing, I tried to mouth that I couldn't hear him, only to have him grin wider and talk even faster. I gave up and just kept nodding and smiling until the song came to an end and the caller announced, "Just need to take a wee break and have a dram or two ourselves to keep up with you peasants!"

"Thank you," I smiled to my dancing companion. He reached down and gave my hand a loud, smacking kiss, making me laugh, before disappearing to the bar, swaying a little as he walked. I looked around me, trying to find Marcus and Jerry over the heads of the crowd. I had lost them a while back now that I thought about it. They had to be here somewhere.

MARCUS AND JERRY were standing near the back entrance. Marcus was giving Jerry a long stare.

"Are you sure? There's a hell of a lot of people here, Jerry."

Jerry paused then nodded firmly. "Aye, I'm sure. We were being watched. Intently. When I looked right at him, he abruptly disappeared."

"Did you get a good look at him?" Marcus urged, his mind racing.

Jerry shook his head in obvious annoyance. "No, he had a hood up, wore dark clothes." He frowned suddenly. "Hang on I might be wrong, but I'm pretty certain I saw a dragon tattoo on one of his wrists. Don't quote me on that."

"Aye, okay. Shit!" Marcus felt frustration and anger bite at him. He had let his guard down for just one damn night and apparently that had been a mistake. Were they not allowed one goddamn night for themselves? Didn't they deserve it? Thank God for Jerry, who no doubt had scared the man off. But who the hell was this man watching them, and more importantly who was he working for? It had to be connected to this case, to Richard, to his mastermind. If Marcus could have taken them all out now, he would have, he was that riled up and raging for this to be done with.

"There you guys are! I was looking everywhere for you. What are you doing standing there?"

Hearing her voice, they both swung their heads round. Sophia was standing there, looking flushed and carefree, grinning at them, happiness slipping out of her eyes. Marcus felt his stomach drop.

Something in their eyes must have alerted her, despite Marcus trying desperately to rearrange his features, because her smile dropped. "What's wrong?"

Sensing Jerry was about to tell Sophia, Marcus squeezed his arm tight to warn him, then stepped up to his wife, plastering on an easy smile. "Nothing, except Jerry having a few too many drams and nearly passing out on the dance floor. I thought it best to get him some wee fresh air." He turned back and gave Jerry a pointed, pleading look.

His sergeant caught on quick, he'd gave him that. "Aye, can't hold my liquor anymore, it seems. What's that all about?"

Sophia gave a laugh, relaxing again. "And you are a true Scotsman too! Honestly, I expected better Jerry. Maybe we should get you both home, huh? Need my arm, Jerry?"

Marcus almost laughed at the expression on Jerry's face. Being considered a lightweight was almost blasphemous in Scotland. But he took it on the chin, taking Sophia's arm, though not before shooting Marcus a black, thunderous look and mouthing "You owe me!" He couldn't argue with that. Still, he couldn't resist adding, tongue-in-cheek, "Need me to take your other arm for you there, old man?" as they made their way out. This time the laugh escaped out as Jerry bit back vehemently, "No!".

Somehow the laughter helped, if only briefly.

Later, curled up behind his sleeping wife, an awake and buzzing Marcus was full of misgivings and doubts. Should he have told Sophia the truth tonight? He'd never lied to her, even when the temptation had been strong to do so. Surely not though, when they weren't even certain this guy was following them. How would he have known where they were? It couldn't be!

No, Jerry must have been mistaken. Better not to have worried Sophia unnecessarily, especially when she had looked so relaxed. But if he was wrong, the fall out of this was terrifying. If this man was following them, and had known exactly where to find them, that meant they were being traced and watched right now, even as Marcus and their team watched them. It meant nowhere was safe for them, not even here in their home, in their bed...

He didn't know then, as he lay in bed fighting against his every gut instinct to convince himself it was a mere coincidence, that later he would curse the fact he didn't tell Sophia. Perhaps then it could have stopped what was about to destroy everything he loved.

Nothing would be as it was for any of them...

[23]

Marcus was still asleep when I stirred. The early morning sunlight streamed through our window as the fog, which had hung like a heavy weight over us for the last few days, finally lifted. After such a good time last night, it felt like a happy continuum. I felt full of renewed determination and faith that the end was in sight, that soon we'd enjoy more fun evenings like last night. I had loved it so much.

The first step in that had been getting Aneella to agree to be wired for the funeral.

As that thought struck me, I had a sudden worry that in all the craziness, no one had told Cathy her daughter was coming to Derek's funeral. Spurred by the realisation, I slipped out of bed, grabbed Marcus' dressing gown and headed into the lounge to find my phone. I knew I would need to be careful to not give away the reason why she'd agreed to do it—it would break Cathy's heart to know that Aneella's reason for going was what she could get out of it —and that I probably should run this past Marcus first. But dammit, she had the right to know!

Mind made up, I finally found my phone on the table and pressed call on Cathy's name.

"Cathy? It's me, Sophia. Sorry to call so early. But I have good news for you!"

A FEW MINUTES LATER, Cathy put the phone down and took in a deep shuddering breath. She wasn't entirely sure how to feel knowing her Ella would be there: relieved, stunned, grateful, happy, pained. So many emotions jostling to come out. Nothing felt quite real... but perhaps nothing was meant to right now. Ella wouldn't be able to come back with her. Cathy wouldn't be able to hold her or bring comfort to her. Her daughter would be under police escort. *Why, oh why did you choose this way, my sweet girl?*

She turned and reached for the silver-framed photo on the mantelpiece of her and Derek on their 25th anniversary, stroking her finger down his face, as her body heaved in grief.

"Our girl is coming; she's coming to say goodbye. I'm grateful for that, my darling. At least we have that. Maybe she's not lost to us after all."

How she prayed for that! *Please God, let her know it's not too late to do something good. I know there's a good heart in there, my beautiful girl.*

Even as she prayed that, a sense of foreboding pressed down on her chest and heart.

IN SHARP CONTRAST, Marcus woke up in a very different frame of mind than his wife, feeling that things were slipping out of his tight control, which was not helped by a hangover from hell. How many drams had he had last night? Clearly a lot more than normal if the banging in his head was anything to go by.

Stumbling around in the bathroom, he searched through the cabinet for some aspirin, or quite frankly, anything that would numb the pain. Maybe arsenic. Finding nothing, he cursed a few times and then did the sensible thing and called out, "Ach, Soph, have you seen the headache tablets?"

No reply.

"Soph?" he tried again, louder, flinching when pain shot through his head.

Silence.

Beginning to feel mildly alarmed, Marcus walked into the lounge. No sign of her. Same story in the kitchen.

Just as he was picking up his phone to call her, alarm now fringing on panic after what had happened last night, he spotted a scribbled note out of the corner of his eye sitting on the work surface and snatched it up.

I'm off to see Cathy to see if she needs any help. I've told her Ella will be at the funeral, but don't worry, I was vague with the details as to why Ella's changed her mind. You looked too peaceful to wake. Love you xx

Now he didn't know whether to feel relieved or even more alarmed. And this damn headache was not helping.

JERRY WAS NURSING A POUNDING headache as he made his way to the police station way too early in the morning for his liking. His shoulders were hunched over, his coat up around his ears against the biting wind, and he wasn't taking much notice of his surroundings. When someone called his name, it took a few moments to filter through to his senses. He turned in the direction of the voice as they said his name again. It was then he got a full view of their face, and his eyes widened in shock, before narrowing as he bit out with an undertone of emotion, "What the hell are you doing here?"

As soon as Cathy opened the door and saw me standing there with warm Danish pastries in my hand, she pulled me into a tight embrace as before. I held her for a long moment. She had lost the two people she loved the most, one through death and one through selfish desires, and I sorely needed a mother figure. When she kissed me on the top of my head before ushering me in, my throat tightened with emotion.

Later, after I'd persuaded her to eat two of the Danishes, noticing that she was getting painfully thin, the conversation turned inevitably to Derek's funeral. Very conscious about what I should and shouldn't say, I steered it towards safer topics and practical arrangements.

"Is there anything I can help you with, any organising?" I asked.

Cathy shook her head, "Having you there is all I need, my dear." There was a pause, a moment suspended where the air hushed itself, before she quietly said, "And my girl, of course. I never thought she would come."

She turned eyes full of deep gratitude onto me. As I sat there struggling with how to respond, feeling guilty and undeserving of her thankfulness, Cathy stood up and walked over to the kettle, presumably to turn it on. Yet as she stood near it, she went very still, her knuckles growing white as she clutched the worktop.

"Cathy?" I gently probed. No answer. Concerned now, I got up from the chair and moved across to her, putting my hand on hers. "Are you alright?"

When still no reply came, I was beginning to think I

might have to shake her shoulders to stir her from this troubling trance, my mind racing as to whether I should call a doctor. In fact, I went to turn her to me, when suddenly her eyes locked onto mine. What I saw darkening those irises made me draw in my breath. Fear. She gripped my hand still covering hers as she whispered, "I have this awful sense something bad is going to happen to my girl. I feel it, here." She pointed at her heart. "And I can't make it go away."

Her voice broke on the last word, and it took everything I had not to let her emotions override my own common sense. Instead, I brought both her hands into mine, and sought to reassure her with a smile and a confidence in my voice: "No, no, nothing's going to happen to Ella. Marcus and his team will keep her safe. We all will," I reassured, squeezing her tight.

And I meant it; I believed it. Of course, Ella would be kept safe. Marcus would never let anyone in his protection come to harm. Nothing would go wrong. He had promised this to me, and he never broke his word.

"It's going to be fine, I promise you."

[24]

M arcus scanned the four faces sitting around the room looking expectantly at him. There weren't many on his team. Sometimes he despaired at how he was meant to crack such a well-established, and therefore powerful, crime ring with so few resources. The two extra officers he'd been allowed to borrow were really there to do admin. Thank God for Jerry. If he lost his inspector, he was absolutely done for, *ann an trioblaid* – *in* serious trouble, up the sodden creek without a sodden paddle.

His head throbbed as if in agreement and Marcus tried not to flinch with the shooting pain. Rubbing his forehead, he tried to arrange his thoughts.

"First of all, I appreciate your patience and under-standing. This hasn't been an easy ride so far. We've all felt at times like there's been little progress. Believe me, I've felt it most. But praise God, we have movement on our new leads. More crucially, Ms. Blair has agreed to be wired up during her father's funeral. So now we need to do everything we can to leak the details of the funeral through the Slyfox codename. Tom, get a message out to the phone number we have identified, using the program codes."

"Yes, Boss."

Marcus nodded then turned to Jerry. "Jerry, we only have surveillance for twenty-four more hours. I want you to make sure we get a firm identity on anyone seen entering and leaving, particularly on the one we believe to be Mr. Rogers."

"On it."

Jerry was standing up and heading out when Marcus called out, "And Jerry, keep an eye out for anyone who matches the description from last night."

They exchanged a look of understanding. Jerry nodded. "Aye, leave it with me."

Marcus gave him a grateful smile. As he headed back to his office, he glanced over at Tom. His young sergeant had barely said two words again today. Something made him backtrack and head over to Tom.

"How are you doing?"

Tom looked startled as he swung his head up. "Uhm... okay, yeah, yep, good."

Marcus titled his head at an angle as he scrutinised the young man's pale features. "Are you sure about that, young Tom? I need you fully focused on this fraud case."

Tom stared at him, then slowly nodded. He sensed again that there was something Tom wanted to say, and paused for a moment, in the hope that it would encourage him to open up. But already the shutters were closing, and that too-bright grin was back. "That I am, thanks, Boss."

Inwardly sighing, Marcus gave him a faint smile, then leaned down and quietly said, "My door is always open," before straightening and turning to head back to his office. As he did, he thought he glimpsed a wet sheen to Tom's eyes.

. . .

As the hour grew late and dusk settled in, Marcus was eager to get home. The headache had finally eased, and he wanted to be in his wife's arms. However, it seemed the universe had other ideas.

"Sir, got a minute?"

He tried not to groan, he really did, when he heard Jerry's voice, but he may have failed. Ach, he was only human.

"Aye, aye, if it's a quick one."

Jerry must have heard the reluctance in Marcus' voice, for he had an apologetic look on his face when his head popped 'round the door.

"I won't keep you long. There's ... ah, someone who wants to see you."

Marcus looked up from turning his computer off, frowning. "Who?"

There was a moment of suspense, then Jerry stepped back with a strange kind of look on his face, and someone else stepped forward.

Andy.

Tom knew he was dragging his feet making his way back to his flat. He also knew he was becoming very good at evading difficult situations, namely one in the shape of Libby. He'd stayed out late last night, knowing she would be asleep by the time he got home, then left at the crack of dawn this morning, though not early enough to avoid his flatmate. He'd slept on the floor and had definitely felt the after-effects this morning, as every muscle ached and protested. The last thing he'd felt like having was an interrogation, but that had been what he'd gotten.

Alex had cornered him by the front door, looking none too happy with his bed hair and hole-ridden t-shirt and boxers.

"Need something there?" Tom had asked in a low voice, keeping a nervous eye on his bedroom door.

"Aye, you could say that!" Alex proclaimed in a loud voice.

"Shh, keep it down, will you," Tom immediately hushed, panicking. "Seriously, man, don't be an eejit. I don't want to wake her."

"I don't give a crap if I do," Alex muttered, though he did lower his voice a little. "Listen, I don't give a shit who you sleep with, but I do have a problem when you move a girl in and she's not paying rent. Got me?"

What could he say? Alex had every right to be unhappy. Tom held up a pleading hand. "I know, I know. I'd be pissed off too. It won't be much longer, yeah? She can't... go home right now. It's not safe—"

"What do you mean it's not safe?" Alex was staring hard at him, looking a tad freaked out. Tom decided to plough on without answering that one. "But I'm going to help find her somewhere to live. Soon." When Alex continued to look unconvinced, he added, "I promise. I'm good for it, you know I am."

"You better, mate, I don't like this."

You and me both.

"Trust me, okay? I'll sort it."

TOM FOUND himself taking a deep breath before turning the key and opening his front door. He couldn't avoid this any longer as much as he wished to God he could. *Never took myself for a coward*, Tom thought humourlessly.

Libby must have heard him for there she was before

him, arms wrapped around her bare midriff, wearing one of his shirts, unbuttoned, over a tank top that swamped her slim frame. He tried not to notice how hot she looked in his clothes.

"Hey," He gave a small smile, walking into the lounge, Libby following close on his heels.

"I thought you were avoiding me."

Tom gave a reluctant laugh. No preamble with her, straight to the point.

He turned to look at her, found himself nodding in a real moment of honesty. "I guess I have been." He shot her an apologetic look.

Libby released her arms, giving him a reluctant smile. "At least you're honest. Most men are lying bastards."

"Yet you're asking me to do something that's totally dishonest. Almost ironic, wouldn't you say?" Tom gave her a pointed look, unable to stop the bitterness seeping into his voice. "You're putting me in an impossible situation, you know that, right?"

Libby looked as if she was about to come out with all those arguments like she'd done before, and Tom tried to steel himself. Yet, maybe she saw something vulnerable in his eyes, for she instead walked closer to him until she was standing right there in front of him, her eyes beseeching him. "I know that. But I've got no one else. If you can't help me, I'm done for."

Tom grabbed her hands. They were icy cold and caused him to shiver a little. Without thinking, he began to rub his thumbs over them in circular motions. "Listen, I've been thinking. We've got more options than we think, aye? We can do this on the right side of the law. We can talk to my boss, see about getting you onto the witness protection program if you testify-"

Libby whipped her hands away as if his touch was

poisonous, halting his rushed-out words. She backed away, shaking her head. Tom felt himself tense up, waiting for the outburst. It was going to be ugly. He was right.

"You're not gonna help me, are you? You lost the nerve to delete my record. You did, didn't you?" When he remained silent, swallowing hard, anger riled inside her eyes, darkening her pupils as she marched up to him. "Thanks for nothing! You've signed my death warrant, you bastard! He's gonna come for me. Why the hell did I think you would be any different?"

He tried to reach for her again, but she fought against him, hitting out in her fear and distress. "Listen, Libby! For the love of God! If I delete your record, it'll be traced back to me. I'll lose my job—"

"That's all you care about—"

"*Then* they will reinstate your record, most likely give you a heavier sentence," Tom ploughed on, desperate to make her understand. "You'll be worse off, and I won't be able to help you 'cause I'll be in jail myself! Listen to what I'm saying here. There's a better way. One that helps you long-term."

Libby was shaking her head, moaning, "I can't testify against him, he will send his mates after me." She swung her head up, her eyes wide. "And then after you. There's no escape."

He couldn't stand looking at those desperate eyes a moment longer. A small, ashamed part of him wanted to bolt, pretend she'd never came to him, pleading for his help. Yet, as he looked down at her, her hands trembling, a larger part of him realised that he wanted to protect her, that his feelings were running crazy for her... and it was this part that won out.

Tom pulled her into his warmth and held her, whispering again and again, "No one is going to hurt you, I'm here," until she stopped fighting and wrapped her arms around him, burying her face in his chest. Then it seemed the most natural thing in the world to raise her head with his fingers under her chin, bend down and kiss her softly, then wait to see if she wanted him to keep kissing her. When she opened her mouth and pressed him against her, he silently sighed in relief, before deepening the kiss. Their breaths were hot and their hands hungry as they pressed up against each other. Something ignited in Tom that never had before when he'd kissed a girl.

It took everything he had to pull back, as her hands found their way under his t-shirt.

"Tom?" she said a little breathless, confused.

"Believe me I want to. You have no idea," Tom groaned a little. "But I don't want to rush this, rush you."

"You're not." She reached up to kiss him again. He couldn't help but kiss her back, wanting to bury himself in her. But something warned him *not yet*. Somehow, he managed to draw away again.

"I'm not going anywhere, Libs," he quietly said. "I'm here for as long as you need me. We don't have to rush anything."

"What are you doing here?"

Everything in him clenched as he stared hard at Andy, who stood there a little hesitantly in the doorway. *Damn right he should be nervous.* Marcus crossed his arms, commenting dryly, "For someone who's been on long-term sick leave, you look remarkably well."

Andy turned around to Jerry, who beckoned impatiently for Andy to move into the room, staying silent. Marcus sensed that Andy being here was not a surprise to his sergeant, and that made him feel that much more annoyed, and yeah, he could admit it hurt that he'd been kept in the dark and now been dropped right in it. Fairly or not, he expected more from Jerry.

"I wanted ..." Andy stopped, then stepped forward, clearing his throat, "I wanted to see if I could come back. Here. I wondered if I could have my old job again on the team." As he finished, he straightened, looking relieved, as well as something unreadable.

"Why?" came Marcus' clipped reply.

"Why?" Andy repeated, looking confused by the question.

"Aye, why now? Six months away is a long time, Andy. A lot can change. You could have changed."

Andy stood there, opening then closing his mouth, too stupefied, it seemed, to form an answer.

"For chrissake, just tell him!" This came from Jerry, who was looking like he was about to explode.

There was a tense, suspended moment, where Marcus found himself holding his breath, before,

"I'm in remission, from cancer. I need to come back while I still can. It might come back at anytime."

Marcus heard that word he loathed—cancer—and froze, then crumbled like a stack of playing cards falling to the ground. Haunting flashbacks of Lucy telling him about her own cancer, the agonising treatment that took everything out of her, only for it to fail and aggressively take her, clouded his mind, making it impossible for him to reply.

He had to swallow hard and compose himself before uncrossing his arms and stepping towards Andy, who stood there barely moving, stiffly holding himself as if unable to allow any emotion to penetrate through his skin. "I wouldn't wish that on anyone, I'm sorry," Marcus quietly said, reaching out to place a hand on Andy's shoulder. Jerry turned away as if unable to watch this display.

That touch seemed to release something in Andy, an emotion sweeping through his eyes. Andy nodded. "Thank you."

"What do you need from me?"

Andy gave his first smile, looking more like the Andy of old. "A job, anything, I don't care what. Literally give me filing if you like. I can't stand another day stuck at home. Any longer or I'm going to go insane."

Marcus gave a faint smile and nodded. He gave Andy's shoulder a quick squeeze, before letting go and pacing the room as he thought hard. Budget was tight, but they were already paying a reduced salary to Andy, so it should be doable if he talked it up right. Andy may have been a little lazy at times, but he was still a skilled sergeant and God knew Marcus needed every person he could get. "I'll need to clear it with HR first, but as soon as I can get you back with us, I will." He stopped in front of Andy, ensuring they had eye contact, before saying, "You have my word."

Andy stared at him, then seeing what he needed to in his boss's eyes, he nodded. "I know you won't let me down, sir. You never do."

[25]

Marcus came in through the front door, gave me an absent-minded smile and a kiss on the cheek as I sat working at my desk, then sat down with a heavy sigh into his favourite worn leather armchair. He leaned back and closed his eyes, weariness seeping out of his every pore. And something more.

Without a word, I went to the kitchen and made us both a coffee, grabbing the bottle of scotch whisky at the last minute.

"Here," I said, holding out the coffee in front of him. When he opened his eyes, I handed him the mug, and when he gave a lukewarm thanks, I held out the whisky. That got a bigger smile, especially when I added a rather generous amount to his coffee. "Ach, now you're talking."

After adding a smaller tipple to my own, I curled up on the end of the sofa near him, waited 'til he was looking at me, then softly asked, "What's wrong?"

It seemed for a long time that he wasn't going to answer. His eyes were looking at me, but his mind was hurtling elsewhere, somewhere that wasn't pleasant, but haunting and painful. It cut me to the quick. I bit down hard to stop myself from saying something inane in a need to take it, whatever it was, away.

Instead, I waited as patiently as I could, and finally he spoke. "There's something I never told you about, something about Lucy."

Those were the last words I expected to hear.

HE WAS BACK in this room but five years before, Lucy sitting where Sophia sat now. He had walked into here, consumed by a terrifying panic he had never felt before nor ever wanted to again. Lucy had been sending a text, but had looked up with a start at the sound of the front door closing.

"Marcus? Why aren't you at work?" There was a confused note to her voice, and a stirring of hesitation.

Marcus came up close, fighting hard to maintain control. He stared at Lucy, clenching and unclenching his fists.

"Is there something you need to tell me?" he said tightly.

Lucy was sitting straighter now, putting down her phone.

"What do you mean?"

"I don't know, maybe start with why your mam felt the need to call me, all concerned about how you were after your doctor's appointment."

She flew up off the sofa, opening her mouth to say something. But he couldn't seem to stop his own words spilling out. "Why would your mam know and not me?"

A big part of him had clung on to the hope her mam had been mistaken. Until he saw the truth in his wife's eyes, and shrivelled and dead, leaving behind a fearfulness in his veins and a gut-wrenching pain in his stomach.

"I'm sorry—I..."

She seemed to be struggling with what to say, how to get the words out. He felt his heart constrict. "Why didn't you tell me if you were worried about something? I would have come with you."

Silence. Lucy turned away. Somehow that was the worst thing she could have done right then, and a cold, awful feeling crept over him. He dragged her back round to face him.

"Why?"

Lucy swallowed, shook her head.

"Why, Lucy? Tell me!"

There were tears in her eyes, spilling out. Marcus cupped her face desperately, not moving an inch, urging her to tell him. The cold was now creeping up his arms and chest.

Then,

"Because I knew this was cancer, the kind you don't get better from. I watched my sister die of the same."

Her words were low, whispered, and he had to strain to hear them. How he wished to God he hadn't.

Every part of his body was pale and cold now. A rise of bile threatened to overwhelm him, and he had to swallow hard. He had to get out of there, before he broke down completely—

Abruptly letting go, Marcus backed away, stumbling for the door. Her faint words, "Wait! Just wait! We need to talk about this!..." faded away the further he ran and ran into the dense woods until his lungs burned in agony and his heart tried to stop breaking into two.

. . .

MARCUS STARED NOW AT NOTHING, still living that dark, awful moment. "I think something broke in me that day. Something that I never quite got back. We never even had time to find our way back to where we were because suddenly, we were in the middle of countless treatments and hospitals appointments."

He heard the hollowness in his voice, loathed the self-depreciation of it, yet couldn't seem to stop it. He couldn't turn to Sophia, see the look in her eyes.

Her voice seemed to come from a faraway place, penetrating through the fog clouding his mind. "What's happened to tell me now?"

A shudder ripped through him. "Andy came in today. God, I've been carrying such bad thoughts about him, believed him to be a liar and deceiver, who turned us over for a better offer." He gave a short humourless laugh. "Ach, you'd think I would stop having such impossible standards for people and give them benefit of the doubt. Maybe I should have done that more with Lucy and then she wouldn't have shut me out..." Marcus closed his eyes. "It turns out Andy's in remission for cancer. All this time I could have been helping him if I'd actually bothered to pick up the damn phone instead of wallowing in my own stupid pride—God, I hate cancer! Will I ever be free of its shadow?"

With that, he hunched over, and began to cry tears he should have wept five years ago.

SHOCKED by all my husband had spilled out, I had sat there through it without moving, desperately trying to make sense of it all, and figure out what I should do or say.

Until I heard his gut-wrenching sobs.

I did the only thing that made sense. I dropped to my

knees before him and drew him tightly into my arms and didn't let go until the last shuddering convulsion had left him and the grief was spent. This man, who had been my stronghold, now clutched me as if I was the only one who could save him from the dark, fierce storm crashing over him. And I fiercely and silently vowed right there and then that I would not shut him out. Not while I still had breath in my lungs and a heart pumping with blood.

RELUCTANTLY, Marcus drew away from the warmth of her arms. He could feel a tinge of embarrassment cursing his cheeks, and he used the palm of his hands to cover his sore, dry eyes for a moment as he said, "Ach, I'm sorry."

Suddenly, his hands were being pulled away, forcing him to stare into the fierce face of his wife.

"Don't ever apologise for crying, you hear me? Or I swear to God..." Her warning trailed off but the smouldering in her eyes remained.

Marcus gave a faint smile. "Aye, aye, I hear you." He pulled her into his lap, settling them more comfortably, wanting the feel of her close to him. Sophia put her arm around his shoulders, her fingers reaching out to bury them into his hair. Her circular movements against his scalp were soothing and he felt some of the tension float away. He may have even given a soft groan of pleasure. Her grin told him he most likely did.

She continued to massage his scalp for a little longer, then quietly said, "Tell me honestly: is this the first time you've allowed yourself to properly grieve for Lucy?"

A long breath escaped from him. He turned to look at her with everything he couldn't say aloud. Her fingers stopped massaging as she absorbed the truth from his eyes then cupped his face and pressed her forehead to his. Her tender gesture almost undid him again. "Oh, Marcus," she sighed. "No one should hold on to pain for that long."

"Perhaps I needed to wait for you to come to me."

"I'm here now."

"Aye, you're here now."

They stayed pressed against each other until Marcus summoned enough courage to ask what had been burning within him. He eased back so he could see her. "I was thinking, we've never talked about starting a family. Would you like to?"

"You have been thinking a lot."

"Aye, too much probably."

Unconsciously he held his breath as a thousand private thoughts he had no access to crossed her features.

At last, she spoke.

"Right now, in this time we are living in, with everything so uncertain and damn hard, I wouldn't, no, because the thought of bringing a child into all of this scares me so much." She rushed on, perhaps hearing his quick intake of breath. "What if we couldn't protect him or her?"

"We would, I would make sure of it."

"But we can't guarantee it, can we?" She looked away, "I don't think I'm strong enough right now to be a good mum, a deserving mum. I will soon, I promise." Sophia nodded quickly, reassuring him.

Marcus nodded too, understanding more than she realised, though a part of him still struggled to believe. Perhaps it was him, perhaps they sensed he would make a rubbish father, as his own had been—

As if reading his black, damaging thoughts, Sophia put her hand on his cheek and smiled. "But when all this crap is behind us, and I'm feeling strong in every way, you'd better be ready to impregnate me, my sexy Scottish warrior, because I can't think of anything I desire more than to be the mother of your bairn."

Relief flooded him, making him feel a little giddy. "I'll make sure the wee swimmers are up for the job. Might need to get them up to their finest form, of course. Apparently, you need to have lots of sex to ensure that." He gave her an exaggerated, suggestive wink.

She laughed. "Is that so? Well, I'm sure we can help them to be ready for the task in hand." There was a brief pause, then, "I tell you something, this child is going to be the luckiest kid to have you as their dad. They are going to be the most loved, most protected, most wanted son or daughter in the whole of Scotland."

He could feel the tears clouding his eyes again, but this time the emotion was soothing and beautiful. He cradled her head. "Thank you," he whispered, before pulling her into a long, deep kiss, showing her how much he loved her the only way he knew how. As he lay her down on the rug, loving her with everything he had, peeling away their clothes 'til there was nothing but the touch of skin on skin, he prayed he could give her the future they both yearned for.

Please God.

[26]

"He keeps calling! He won't leave me alone!"

Tom had just walked into the flat and closed the door when Libby was in front of him, clutching her phone, a frantic look in her eyes. He suppressed a weary sigh and started moving into the kitchen, feeling a sudden urge for an ice-cold beer.

"Who won't?" he asked while reaching into the fridge to draw out a much-needed drink, pressing it against his pounding head for a brief, sweet moment, before reaching for the bottle opener.

"Who do you think?" She had followed him into the room, watching him impatiently as he greedily drank half of it in one desperate go.

Jake. Tom sagged against the fridge. Of course, she had meant Jake. Like there could be anything else in their lives right now. "Did you answer?"

"Are you pissing me right now? Of course I didn't!"

Tom rubbed his forehead, grimacing. "Any chance you could answer me without shouting? Please," he added as she shot him a look that could burn holes into his skull. "I get that you're pissed and scared right now, okay? I get it. But I've had a long day, and tomorrow, well it's going to be even worse. I'm knackered, like I could sleep right here standing up." He closed his eyes as if to prove it.

Silence. Utter, blessed silence.

"Sorry."

That had him stunned. She never apologised. Ever. Libby stepped closer, biting her lip. "I'm sorry, okay? I know you didn't ask for any of this bullshit in your life. You're about the only friend I have right now. I don't want to lose you."

There was a rawness in her eyes that moved him. Tom reached out and took her hand, tugging her closer. "You're not going to lose me."

He held her gaze, and it seemed to be enough to convince her. Suddenly, he found her mouth on his, pressing hard, demanding a response he couldn't help but give. His hands wrapped around her hips and the small of her back, where her tank top stopped, and there was only warm soft skin below. Arousal stirred between them as her mouth opened for him. His hands moved of their own accord, lowering closer to her ass as she pressed up tight against him. More and more he was questioning his insane decision to hold them off from giving in to what they both wanted. In fact, he was about to say so when just as sudden as it began, the warmth of her body was gone, and his arms were holding nothing but cool air.

"I'll make you some food."

"What?" He looked at her a bit dazed, as Libby began looking in the cupboards. "Lib, you don't cook."

She found a can of baked beans and pointed it at him with a smile. "I'm pretty sure I could make you baked beans on toast without messing it up... Uh, how do you open the can?"

Tom shook his head, laughing as he searched for the can opener. He held it out to her with a small grin. "This might help."

Libby took it from his hand with a look of perplexity in her eyes: "Ah... okay, yeah." He waited, expecting her next question and sure enough: "How do I use it?"

MUCH LATER, they were curled up together in bed, her back to him, the two of them only touching where his arm was wrapped around her waist. She was wearing one of his t-shirts and, he prayed to God, some knickers too, because the thought of her without... He'd purposely kept on a vest top and boxers on and was trying to keep everything under control, and he did mean everything. There was a reason he was keeping a distance between their bodies, especially in the lower region, and it was taking every ounce of self-control he could squeeze out.

But it seemed Libby wasn't getting the message. Or didn't want to, it was impossible to tell. She inched back until her bottom was pressed tight against him, bringing his arm tighter around her, until it grazed her breasts. Tom felt his body jolt and couldn't seem to stop his mouth dropping to kiss her neck and along her jawline. Her arm reached back and circled his neck, dropping her head back to give him greater access. Everything within him went into meltdown and he let instinct take over. He moved one hand up to cover her breasts, and the other to stroke her stomach and thighs. She gave a soft moan, then turned her head so their mouths could meet in a deep kiss, as she rocked against him, and he against her.

Tom turned her so she was lying on her back, deepening the kiss, covering the length of her body with his. Even half-mad with need, something made him stop and look at her intently. She frowned, trying to draw him back to her. He cradled her face, stilling her. He needed to know. She had been used so many times, treated like dirt. He never wanted to make her feel like that.

"Are you sure? Is this what you want?"

Libby widened her eyes at his soft, urgent question, her face softening into a smile as she reached up and touched his lips with her fingers. She reached up and pulled her t-shirt off, throwing it on the floor.

"I'm going to take that as a yes," Tom managed to breathe before sliding down and taking her nipple into his mouth, wanting everything, every touch, every part of her. He felt her pulling off his clothes with almost trembling fingers. That got him. He took a deep breath to slow himself down, gentled his hands, and tenderly stroked her till she stopped trembling and took him into her, showing her in the only way he knew how what it was to give yourself to another, and be loved in return.

THEY WERE DRIFTING off to sleep, Libby warm and settled in his arms, when the demanding vibration of her phone on the bedside table jerked them awake. Libby scrambled up to grab it as Tom bolted up to a sitting position. When she saw the caller ID, her face went as pale as the moonlight streaming in through his bedroom window.

"Is it him?" Tom uttered as every part of him went rigid in anticipation.

Libby nodded. Their eyes met, and the fear he saw in her wide dark pupils snapped something dangerous in him.

"Let me have the phone." Not giving her much option in it, he took it off her and immediately hit accept. "Leave her the hell alone. Or I swear to God..."

"Or what, you dickhead?" Jake's voice was cocky and

cold. "Think you scare me, pussy? The bitch lost me money, and she needs to pay up. Unless you want to pay up for your whore."

Hearing Jake call Libby a whore and a bitch, to have her threatened by this prick of a moron, had the rage landing like a red mist over him. "Yeah, let's meet, you bastard, right now! Give me an address."

Libby was frantically shaking her head, trying to take the phone back from him, but Tom grimly held her off. Jake said in a cold sneer, "Back of the park where we used to hang out. Ten minutes. Remember it, Tommy boy? And you'd better be alone with none of your police buddies with you or she'll be paying the price."

The phone went dead. Tom dropped it as if it had burned him, then leaped off to yank on his clothes. Libby was off the bed and trying to stop him, blocking his way.

"You can't meet him! Have you lost your mind?! He'll kill you—"

"No, he won't. He... won't, alright?" He pressed her down onto the bed, then reached for his shoes. "We are not doing this anymore, letting him have all the control, threatening you—I'm done with it!"

Libby moved onto her knees, hugging herself. "But what're you going to do?"

Not a frickin' clue. If he allowed himself to think about the insanity of what he was doing here, well...

"I'll think of something. Stay here."

He moved to the door.

"Tom!"

Tom paused, turned his head to look at her. She was still in the same position, clutching the sheet to her naked body. "You better come back to me, you hear me? Or I'll bloody kill you myself. I need you."

He swallowed, nodded once, then was gone.

. . .

THE STREETS WERE EERILY silent around the city as Tom parked near the park, looking apprehensively around him. The inky black night seemed to enclose him. Memories of his childhood spent in this estate came rushing back. Jake had been an alright person back then. They used to get up to no good, but never harmed anyone. They were never aggressive. Until Jake discovered drugs and started selling and taking them a year back. Now the chemicals had messed with his brain and turned him into a violent thug who cared about no one. Tom bitterly regretted the day he'd introduced Libby to him. God, if he had known...

The initial anger driving him had dissipated, and that wasn't good at all. Fear was trying to creep in, or maybe his sixth sense screaming at him that this night was not going to end well. In fact, this was probably the most idiotic thing he'd ever done, and there were a lot of stupid things racked up against his name trying to claim that prize.

What would Marcus do? He'd leave a trail. Tom grabbed his phone and hammered out a text to Jerry with his location, adding:

IF YOU DON'T HEAR from me in an hour, get here. I'm about to do something stupid, but I have to do it to protect someone. Before you come for me, go to my flat first and make sure Libby is safe. Tell her I sent you.

AS HE PRESSED SEND, he looked up to see Jake, leering at him. He appeared to be alone, but Tom wasn't fooled for a minute. His mates would be there in the shadows.

Taking a shuddering breath, Tom got out of his car and walked towards Jake, trying to appear confident.

"Didn't think you had it in you to turn up," Jake sneered.

"There's a lot you don't know about me anymore," Tom replied, walking up until they were close enough that he could see the ravages of the drug use on Jake's face, the dead look in the eyes that had once sparked with humour and light. Tom put up his hands. "I just want to talk. This shit has got to stop. You've got to leave Libby alone, man."

Jake's eyes narrowed. "I haven't got to do anything, asshole. That bitch owes me. And one of you is gonna pay up."

"And if we paid you, what then, huh? You're gonna keep coming back and back." He shook his head. "That isn't happening. Full stop."

Jake grabbed Tom's shirt, his fist clenching tight. "Do not piss me off! Otherwise, I'm going to send my boys straight to your flat and they ain't going to play nice."

Acute, sickening fear ripped through him. Tom fought against showing it on his face and forced himself to continue to look Jake boldly in the eye. He said as calmly as he could, "They'd be wasting their time, seeing as she's not there. Tell me, what the hell happened to you, eh? How did my former mate turn into just another no-good piece of shit who's going to end up dead or in prison, huh?"

He could sense he was being enclosed, surrounded by other dark shadows as the rage in Jake's eyes threatened to burn him alive. And still he kept taunting, because the longer Jake wanted to kick the living daylights out of him, the less he would think about sending his mates to where Libby was. That was all that mattered.

"Really, I'm curious how you decided, you little shit-brained wanker, to give me the chance to send your sorry arse into prison. And believe me, I'm going to, you and your little friends hiding away back there, where you'll have to wipe the crap off the floor I'll walk on—"

He had tried to brace himself, but that first blow to his stomach, delivered by a screaming, cursing Jake, had him doubled over, the air rushing out of him so fast that he had to fight to breathe. Then the kicks came, and everything became a pain-induced blur as he allowed himself to become the sacrifice...

MARCUS WAS ALMOST DRIFTING off to sleep when his mobile vibrated loudly. Fumbling to find it on the table next to him, he peered at the name, trying to clear his blurry eyes. Jerry.

Stifling a sigh, he answered it, sitting up as he did. Aware that Sophia was asleep next to him, he padded silently out of the room, grabbing his dressing gown as he did. Somehow it felt a little odd to be talking to his sergeant butt-naked.

"Jerry, this had better be good."

Marcus could hear the siren in the background, and rushed voices, before Jerry said in a distressed voice, "It's Tom. He's been badly beaten up. It's not good, I'm going to the hospital now."

He found himself speechless for a moment, as he swayed on the spot. His young sergeant; what the hell had happened?

"Aye, aye, okay. I'll meet you there."

"Okay, sir." Jerry hung up.

Marcus rubbed his face, trying to compose himself, then hurried into the bedroom to fling some clothes on. Sophia, who has still been half-asleep, now stirred and sat up.

"What's happened? Where are you going?"

Marcus looked over to her as he pulled on a sweater. "It's Tom, he's been badly hurt."

That had her wide awake, covering her mouth in alarm. "Oh no! Can I do anything?"

He reached across the bed to give her a quick kiss and softly said, "Pray. Pray with everything you've got that the young boy is saved."

[27]

By the time Marcus arrived at Raigmore Hospital, despite unashamedly blue-lighting it all the way, Tom had already been moved to ICU and heavily sedated. Jerry was waiting for him, looking ashen and shaken, and Marcus got him a sweet tea and guided him to a seat.

After Jerry had taken a few sips, and seemed to have more colour in his cheeks, Marcus quietly said, "Do we know what happened, why he was attacked?"

Jerry shook his head. "Only what he put in his text to me. Here." He opened it up on his phone, then passed it to Marcus. "That's as much as I know, but I wish to God he'd confided in me before this, that I do."

"You and me both." Marcus shook his head grimly, staring at the text. "At least he had enough common sense to text you." He frowned suddenly then looked up in alarm. "Who's Libby? Tom's obviously concerned about her. We should get patrol to check on her—"

"Already done, sir. I did that before going to find Tom. She's being looked after by our officers."

Marcus let out a relieved breath. "Good, good. We'll talk

to her soon." He turned to look towards the window into ICU. Tom was lying in the far bed, not moving, tubes attached to his hand. Marcus swallowed. "How is he? What have the doctors said?"

Marcus turned back to Jerry, who was sitting immobile, his eyes troubled.

"Not good," Jerry finally said, "he's not good at all."

Marcus swore under his breath. "I knew something was wrong. I knew it and I let it slide. I figured he would tell me when he was ready." Marcus grimaced. "If anything happens to him..."

Jerry leaned forward. "You're not alone in that. I'm as much to blame."

Marcus moved his head back towards where his young sergeant lay. "One thing's for sure. We need to make sure one of us is checking on him from now on."

A FEW AGONISING HOURS LATER, and Marcus was coming off the phone to Sophia when Jerry came racing around the corner of the corridor.

"He's awake!"

"Thank God," Marcus breathed, before swiftly following Jerry back to ICU. After donning mask and gown, they walked over to where Tom lay. Marcus had to control his facial features not to react upon seeing the badly swollen and bloodied face of his sergeant. One eye was partially closed and the other was looking at him anxiously. Next to him, Marcus heard Jerry curse softly.

Marcus took the seat near the bed as Tom croaked urgently, "Is Libby okay? Is she alright-"

"Aye, aye," he quickly hastened to assure, touching Tom's arm, "she's being taken care of by our team. Jerry here organised it."

Jerry nodded. "I made sure, Tom, as soon as I got your text."

Tom's one good eye closed in vivid relief. "Thank you. I know, God I know, I messed up big time going to meet Jake without backup, using police time to look up Libby and Jake on the system. I thought I could solve this by myself, but all I did was put Libby and me in danger." His eyes turned and pleaded to them both. "I'm sorry, so sorry. I let you down, and your trust in me..."

There was a moment of silence as they all digested this, then Marcus gently said, "Tom, we all mess up in the heat of our emotions. You've learnt from this, you won't make the same mistake again, aye? It's what you do now that matters. I need you to tell me who Libby is, and what exactly's been going on, and who did this to you. Don't leave any detail out." He leaned closer, looking at him squarely in the eye. "You need to trust me now. I promise not to judge."

Tom stared at Marcus, then slowly nodded, his Adam's apple bobbing up and down as he clearly fought to control his emotions. Right then, he looked so small and vulnerable that Marcus wanted to hold him in his arms.

Instead, he listened without interrupting, his mind racing even as he appeared calm and composed outwardly. After Tom had finished, Marcus turned to Jerry.

"Jerry, get an immediate arrest warrant out for Jake— Tom, what's his surname?"

"Ramsay."

"Jake Ramsay." He glanced back at Tom. "As he already has a record in the system, he won't get bail."

Jerry gave a quick nod and stood. "Consider it done." He reached down and gently squeezed Tom's shoulder. "Rest up, son. We need you back on the team."

After Jerry had gone, Marcus gave a faint smile. "He's

right, we need you. Don't ever think we don't. We work as a team, trusting the other. That means we're honest with each other and share our troubles. Understood?"

Tom nodded, then half-whispered, before asking what was obviously burning away at him. "What happens now?"

"For Libby? She'll go into witness protection and be called to testify against Jake." Marcus said, watching Tom closely. They both knew what that meant. Libby would be given a new identity and moved far away, set up with a new job and flat... and for her sake leave Tom behind.

A wash of evident pain mixed with overwhelming relief swept over the young man, moving Marcus. What he must have been going through these last few weeks...

"Will I... will I get a chance to say goodbye?"

He loves her.

Conflict tore at him, and Marcus found himself speaking against his better judgement. "I'll see what strings I can pull, but no promises."

Tom let out a long breath. "Thank you, boss."

He suddenly looked exhausted and a little pale. Marcus stood up. "I'm going to let you rest." As he moved to go, Tom's voice floated over to him. "Give them hell today, at you know where. Catch the bastards."

He meant at Derek's funeral, Operation Slyfox, as it had been named. Marcus gave a half-smile. "Aye, we'll do our best. Wish us luck, have a feeling we're going to need every wee drop going."

[28]

It felt strange to be waking up alone. Disconcerting even, to realise how quickly you've become part of a couple, to the point that nothing feels quite right without them near you, breathing the same air as you.

Today, more than ever, I didn't want to be here by myself. I knew it was going to be hard in so many ways, not only for Cathy saying her final goodbye to the love of her life, but knowing everyone there, especially Aneella, was in potential danger because we were trying to draw out those behind the criminal ring. Though she had lost my love and trust when she betrayed me, that didn't mean I wanted any harm to come to her. That would be too horrendous to even contemplate. Cathy couldn't take any more heartache. We had to keep Aneella safe, no matter what.

The sky outside seemed to share my conflicting thoughts, heavy with grey clouds one minute, then a ray of sunlight breaking through the next, alighting the vivid purple heather. I would have given anything to go walking amongst the woods right now.

Marcus had called earlier, updating me on Tom's condition, and asking me to come directly to the church so I could be there when his officers arrived with Aneella. He'd stopped trying to convince me not to come, understanding there would be no changing my mind. Right now, he was on his way to the prison to get Aneella wired up. As I zipped up my black dress, Tom suddenly crossed my mind, distracting me from my disconcerting thoughts. Poor guy, what a high price to pay for trying to help a friend, even if he did go about it all wrong. Thank God he was going to be okay. Marcus would have blamed himself for not stopping it, even though there was no way he could have known.

Ten minutes later, I stood ready with my shoes and coat on, trying to stay calm as I kept one eye on the clock. Why did I feel so odd, every breath a struggle? I closed my eyes and forced myself to take slow breaths in and out to get myself under control.

It's going to be okay, it's all going to be okay....

THE CHURCH HAD a few people mingling about when I arrived. Cathy was standing to the side, twisting her hands anxiously. I tried to catch her eye and, failing that, was about to go over, when a hand reached out to stop me. Startled, I looked up and into the tired, blue eyes of my husband. He must have changed into the suit jacket he kept spare at the office, as I didn't recognise it, and it looked a little on the crumpled side.

Marcus pulled us into a small alcove, sheltering me from view. I reached up to briefly touch his cheek. "Are you okay?" I murmured.

He gave me a faint smile. "Ach, ask me that again in a few hours. No time to consider that now." His voice suddenly dropped, and he leaned closer to my ear. "Listen, stay as close to me as you can, and a distance from Aneella."

I frowned. "I need to support Cathy and if she's standing close to Ella then—"

"Please, *mo leannan*." There was an urgency in his voice as he stared down at me, grabbing my shoulders almost painfully. "Do this for me. I can't be worrying about you too."

I wasn't sure I could keep to what he said, but I found myself nodding, if only to take that look out of his eyes. "Okay, I'll try my hardest to."

Marcus relaxed his hold, evident relief in his eyes. "Thank you." He cradled my face then gave me a quick kiss. He was about to pull away when I tugged at his hands. He gave me a quizzical look. "Promise me you'll keep her safe," I pleaded. "Promise me."

He seemed to hesitate, his expression hard to read, before saying what I needed to hear. "I promise."

I sensed her walk into the room. The hairs on the back of my neck stood up, and my body grew still even as my heart beat harder in my chest. For one strange moment, I couldn't seem to move, then slowly I turned to face the doorway. She was looking directly at me, that slightly mocking look in her eyes. Once, I would have immediately looked down, but now I steadfastly held her gaze. The slight smile tainting her lips told me that she begrudgingly admired me for it. Then Aneella was being led to the front of the church by the two officers flanking her, where Cathy was waiting, looking at her daughter with a heart-breaking love that threatened to be my undoing.

I watched as mother and daughter stared at each other, a thousand words unsaid. Then Cathy gave a sob and pulled Aneella into her arms, despite the handcuffs making it impossible for Ella to hug her back, and the startled officers standing guard unsure how to respond. I watched as Ella tried to hold herself together, stiff in the embrace. And then I watched as Ella squeezed her eyes shut with a quiet cry and dropped her head onto her mother's shoulder, her body shaking with tremors as she fought against a tide of emotion. Tears blurring my vision, I had to turn away. As I did, I felt a warmth spreading over to me from where Marcus stood in the shadows, keeping watch over us all. My phone buzzed, and I looked down at it.

'Stay strong. I love you. M xx'

Keeping my head bent, a surprised smile lighting my face, I texted back: 'I love you too my Scottish warrior xx'

The vicar was encouraging us to sit down. A few more people had arrived. Were they here as friends... or enemies?

JERRY AND MARCUS exchanged frustrated glances from their opposite places across the church. So far, no one was arousing suspicion, all sitting quietly and respectfully as the service was conducted by the softly spoken vicar. Only the occasional sound of quiet weeping from the front of the church. Andy, dressed undercover along with a couple of officers, gave Marcus a small shrug, as bemused as they all were.

Dammit it to hell! Had they worked out that the message had been a trap?

He couldn't even consider the option that they might fail, not when he'd had to beg for the resources and money to do this. Then there was Glasgow office, who were not happy being side-lined on this, and would have his bollocks for breakfast if he got this wrong.

The service was ending, the pallbearers preparing to move the coffin to the graveyard outside. Aneella and Cathy were standing up, the former giving him a hard stare as she turned to face them, her accusing eyes burning into him.

And still nobody made a move

I WATCHED them lift Derek's coffin up, taking him far away from his family to a place they couldn't follow. Cathy reached out for her daughter's hand; only to stop and stare at the handcuffs around Aneella's hands.

As if sensing her mum's growing distress, Aneella turned and allowed their eyes to connect for the first time that day. Cathy took an involuntary step back in shock, covering her mouth. Ella went to lift her hands as if to reach for her mum, then bit back a frustrated sigh when the handcuffs prevented her.

"Mum?"

Cathy shook her head, "Oh, my darling girl." She reached up to cradle Ella's cheek, her hand trembling a little. "What happened to you, to make you hate the world so much?"

Aneella started, her rigid mask slipping. Yet she remained silent, pressing her lips together as if afraid to say anything.

"Can you not find the light again?" Cathy whispered.

Aneella squeezed her eyes shut, as if unable to look at her. "It's too late." Opening them again, her eyes were awash with surprising regret. "I'm sorry we've both broken your heart. I'm sorry I can't be the daughter you deserve. Take Sophia instead. Forget about me. Please."

With that, she stepped back until Cathy's hand dropped away. "What are you saying?" She gasped. "You're my daughter, always, no matter what! I love you. I..."

The vicar cleared his throat. They both turned in a daze to him. "The pallbearers are ready, Mrs Blair, when you are," he murmured.

"Of course, of course. We're so sorry." Cathy tried to smile at him.

"No need to apologise."

At his signal, the pallbearers lifted the coffin and slowly, respectfully, began to walk down the aisle. Cathy and Aneella filed in behind, and the rest of the small gathering of people followed, including me.

[29]

A biting wind caught the pallbearers by surprise, almost knocking them off their feet with its force as they walked out of the church entrance and into the grave-yard. It had recently rained and left a bright gleam to the ground, causing the mourners to blink their eyes after the subdued light of the church.

I followed a little distance behind Cathy and Ella, trying to heed Marcus' request to do so. But it was so hard not to move closer. I wanted to go up and take Cathy's arm and support her. And for Ella ... well I didn't know what I wanted to do when it came to her, but what was new there? Who had ever understood what she needed? Did she even know herself?

My eyes casting a quick sweep around me as we gathered around the grave prepared for Derek, my hair whipping my face though I tried to tame it back, I caught sight of where Marcus was, along with his undercover officers dressed as other mourners positioned strategically around. I tried not to make eye contact with them and instead focused on the coffin as it was carefully lowered into the ground. For the briefest moment, my mind went back to the last time I had seen Derek, lying unmoving on his bed, following my movements with his eyes as if desperate to communicate with us. My heart had gripped for him then. Now it broke for him.

"Rest in peace, Derek," I whispered. "You've earned an eternity of it."

There was a thud as the coffin touched the earth. The vicar began to recite the last rites. And all the while, my stomach clenched with the thought that any minute now, Marcus might spot a possible leader of the criminal ring and jump into action with no thought to his own safety. Yet what other choice did we have? We'd made our decision, now we had to see it through.

THERE WAS interference on the earbuds, the frequency crackling, no doubt caused by the strong wind. Marcus frowned as he discreetly pressed his ear, hoping to clear it. "Can everyone still hear me? Give me a nod if you do," he said into the mic tucked inside his jacket. He swiftly looked up to see Jerry, Andy and four undercover officers give a quick nod. "Good. Ms. Blair, can you hear me?"

He watched her look up from where she stood by the graveside as the vicar made the sign of the cross. Aneella then turned her head to one side. "Yeah, I can, but I'm a little preoccupied to chat right now. Why don't you concentrate on keeping me alive instead, i.e. your job."

Marcus was surprised his earpiece didn't catch fire with the ferocity that was delivered down the wire. He grimaced but refrained from replying.

He had that eerie sense they were being watched, his detective skills kicking into overdrive. But as he scanned the area and the onlookers for the hundredth time, all was exactly as it had been since they had arrived at the grave-side. Cathy was now stepping forward to drop a rose on top of the coffin and they only had minutes left. Frustration bit away at him. *Come on, show yourselves!*

Wait, hold on. Aneella was looking behind her in an agitated manner. "Ms. Blair, what's happening? Talk to me!" he commanded, as he began to weave through the press of people to reach her.

There was a crackling sound but nothing else. All at once, she was moving, taking him by surprise.

"Ms. Blair! What are you doing?" he practically shouted. Jerry had already sprung into action and was searching the outer rim. "Andy, get over to Ms. Blair!"

Andy remained still, as if he hadn't heard, looking in the opposite direction from Marcus so Marcus couldn't even signal to him. Now Aneella was coming up close to Sophia and seemed to be heading straight for her. *Dammit, what the hell was going on?* Were the earpieces working? The wind had picked up again, and it was impossible to know. He was starting to walk quickly now, only one thought on his mind: to get to Sophia before Aneella did, to act as a human shield if needed.

"They're here. They're coming! You need to protect me!" Aneella's voice practically screamed through his earpiece.

Marcus swore, roughly waving to his officers to move towards the outer rim of the mourners. "Ms. Blair, stop moving! Jerry and Hamish, get yourself over there. Andy, move!"

He was nearly there himself now, pushing through bodies. He caught flashes of Sophia staring at him, then Aneella, aware that something was wrong, very wrong. Still Andy didn't move. He was almost in reaching distance—

Everything seemed to slow down as he fought to react.

A glimpse of an unrecognised man from the shadows, the glint of metal in his hand... A cry... Officers pushing people back... Sophia gasping as Aneella flung herself towards her... His own voice shouting "Get down!" ... Screams as a gunfire split the air... Aneella collapsing into Sophia's arms as they both fell.

Then everything moved fast. Everyone was running in panic, his officers sprinting after the unknown man. Jerry was gently moving Aneella, who had become dead weight on top of Sophia. Marcus flew to the ground before them, cursing. Jerry started to check Aneella over. Cathy was crying next to him, asking him, "Are they okay?" but he had to block her out because Sophia was covered in seeping blood, white-faced and clearly in shock. He began running hands over his wife. "Tell me where you are bleeding from," he urged, trying to stem the panic building in him.

Sophia shook her head, desperately trying to pull herself together. "It's not me. It's not my blood."

"Are you sure?" Marcus had to make sure, his heart still beating frantically.

Sophia nodded, then became aware that Aneella was lying on the ground, still. She scrambled over to her. "Ella? Ella! Stay with us! Help her, Marcus!" she pleaded, reaching up to hold back a sobbing Cathy who was trying to rouse her daughter in near panic.

He leaned over Aneella to check if she was breathing. "Thank God, she is " he thought, though it was shallow. "She's breathing. Jerry, call an ambulance, now!"

Blood was oozing from the gunshot in her spleen area and soaking the ground. He pulled off his coat to try to stem it. Aneella gave a soft moan, and Sophia bent down to whisper comforting words into her ear, stroking back her hair in a loving way that made Marcus want to weep. He indicated for Jerry and quietly murmured, "Get Sophia out of here."

Jerry nodded, then pulled a protesting Sophia away.

As he used the rest of his coat to cover Aneella to keep her core body temperature up, all he could think, over and over till the words were screaming at him, was - *she can't die, she can't! Sophia would never forgive me.*

[30]

S omeone had managed to find some spare clothes for me to change into, which I was grateful for. The metallic smell of Aneella's blood staining me had begun to make me feel queasy, once the initial shock had worn off. My stomach felt like it was on a rocky boat, unable to find solid ground. Having Ella collapse like a dead weight on me was something I would never forget. It would be etched forever in my mind, like a searing wound. And that horren-dous sound of gunfire... I swear I could still hear it blasting in my ears.

The hospital waiting area felt stuffy and airless, and I fought the urge to escape outside for a few moments. Cathy needed me here. I turned to gaze at her sitting next to me on the hard, unforgiving chairs. She was staring straight ahead without moving, as if by keeping still, she would somehow affect the outcome. I wasn't sure if she was even aware I was there. Yet when I shifted slightly in my seat to try to ease an ache spreading in my lower back, she shot a hand out to cover mine, which was resting on the armrest between us. My other warm hand covered her cold one. Above us the clock ticked loudly as if reminding us that any minute now, everything could change.

Marcus had disappeared some time ago, God knew where, which quite frankly was probably for the best. I was fighting a raw, forceful emotion that I couldn't even put a name to. It was more than anger, more than disappointment, but something else entirely that seared within me. For the first time ever, Marcus had broken a promise to me: he hadn't kept her safe. *He hadn't kept her safe.* I knew if I had been thinking rationally, I would think I was being unfair, that I knew how many hours he had put into ensuring every safety precaution was put into place. But right now, I was a long way from feeling rational, not when I was sitting beside a woman who had just buried her husband, then watched in horror as her only child was shot in front of her. Marcus and I hadn't spoken two words since we'd arrived. Until we had more news, that was exactly how I planned to keep it.

The minutes ticked, longer and louder, and still we waited, as the oblivious world around us continued as it had.

JERRY, who had just arrived from the crime scene, was looking at Marcus in a way that made Marcus feel on edge, as if he was expecting his boss to have a full-on panic attack at any minute. Hell, it wasn't far from the truth. Marcus could feel the clammy sweat on his forehead and his palms as he paced back and forth, waiting for the doctor to come out of the room. He was acutely aware that he was avoiding his wife in the next corridor down, like some miserable coward. Usually, one look from her warmed his whole being. But that look she'd given him when they had first come into the hospital had sent a cold shiver down his spine.

To distract himself, he started throwing questions at Jerry.

"Area cordoned off and forensics on scene?"

"Aye. We should have a report by the end of the day."

"Have all the witnesses been questioned?"

"The majority of them. Our officers should be done in the next hour."

"Anything of significance? Any positive ID on the shooter?"

Marcus had stopped pacing now and was staring hard at Jerry. He was also desperately praying as never before. *Let there be something to salvage from this unholy mess.*

Jerry hesitated and Marcus had all the answer he needed, even before his sergeant gave a brief shake to his head. "Not yet. But it's early days."

They both knew Jerry was sugarcoating the otherwise stark reality. Biting back a curse, Marcus begun pacing again.

"The bullet removed from Ms Blair is being sent to forensics team. Make sure they get it, will you Jerry?"

"I will. Any news yet on Ms. Blair's condition?"

Marcus stilled as he looked at Jerry, his hands unconsciously clenching by his side. "She's in the operating theatre. It's all just a sodding waiting game."

A moment of grim silence, then Jerry said, "You know Glasgow will be after our necks."

Marcus shook his head. "No, no: my neck alone, and I'll make sure of that. This was my decision, my cock-up, not yours or that of anyone else on the team, and I'll take the full blame."

Jerry was about to say something, looking troubled, when the drawn doctor emerged from the swinging double doors, and paused when he saw them. Marcus and Jerry stepped up to him, their breaths held tight.

As soon as we saw the doctor walking towards us, with Marcus and Jerry following close behind, we leapt up. Cathy was staring pleadingly at the doctor, but I could only look at my husband. Why was he avoiding my eyes, looking anywhere but at me? He never did that. Ever. Not with me, not with anyone.

And in that dark moment, as his jaw grimly clenched, I knew, I knew. Oh god I knew. Yet even as the doctor was saying how sorry he was, that there was nothing they could do, even as Cathy let out a piercing wail that would haunt me forever, I still refused to believe it. *I can feel you, Ella! I feel you. You can't be dead, you can't! Not you. This isn't what I wanted.*

Everything began to spin, and I forced myself to inhale in, even as I tried to hold back a cry.

I was vaguely aware of Marcus asking if we could see Aneella, of the doctor hesitating, then shaking his head and saying it wasn't possible. Dimly, I could hear the disbelief and rising anger in Marcus's voice as he responded and Jerry's protest. The harrowing cries of Cathy reached somewhere in my soul.

But what I heard, with an ever-growing resounding beat in my head, growing louder and louder by the second, was her last words, trickling like tar through my veins. *"If anything happens to me, it will be on you. And that guilt knowing it was down to you I was harmed... will break you, my darling Sophia. It will break you apart."*

[31]

The next few hours were a living nightmare.

Marcus found himself in a raging battle. He was trying to get himself and his forensic team to see Aneella's body, only to be met with continual denial. He felt like he was losing his mind. They were claiming the body had already been taken to Glasgow. By whose permission, they wouldn't say. Hours later, trying to call in every favour he could, he still had no idea the exact location of her body. *Just what the hell was going on?* Her grieving mother, Cathy, had had to be treated for shock and was taken to a close friend's house rather than allowed home. He'd never seen someone turn the colour of death like that before.

As for his wife, she had not spoken one word to him these last hours, and it was tearing him up inside, along with the crucifying guilt of Aneella's death. It was why he hadn't been able to look at her in the eyes, unable to bear the accusation that must have been there when they delivered the news.

He'd let her down. He'd let them all down.

Marcus walked slowly through the police station bull

pit, which was mercifully quiet, as his men were scattered elsewhere. He reached his office, shut his door, then wearily dropped into his chair, leaning forward to let his head fall into his hands. His body felt numb, crushingly drained, and he had the strongest desire to fall into a dreamless sleep and pretend none of this was happening for a few sweet hours.

The door swung open. Marcus lifted his head. "Can it wait-"

"No, lad, it can't."

Hearing the deep, familiar voice, Marcus sprang up, coming around the desk as Jackson and another plain-clothed officer walked in as if they owned the room. Frowning deeply, Marcus eyed them both. Inside his head, alarm bells were going off.

"Chief Inspector Jackson, I... wasn't expecting you."

Jackson raised a bushy grey eyebrow as the other younger officer gave a snort as if amused, which Marcus did his best to ignore. "Weren't you? I find that hard to believe, seeing as you've made a total pissing cock-up of the first degree with the case that's fast becoming an embarrassment to the force."

Jackson sat down on a chair, crossing his legs. His silent, smirking partner leaned against the wall, arms crossed, as he watched Marcus in a way that made Marcus want to punch him in the face. God, he was more on edge than he'd realised.

Watching them both carefully, Marcus took a moment to compose himself, before saying as calmly as he could, "This cock-up, as you call it, will be straightened out by me. I made the decision to carry out it, so I'll be the one to shoulder the responsibility."

Jackson, rubbing his clean-shaven cheek, cocked his head as he studied Marcus. "You're young to be a DI. Our friend over there, Hobson, is about your age. He dreams of climbing the ladder to DI, don't you, my son?"

Hobson merely gave a nod as he leaned nonchalantly against the wall.

"It seems you had someone on your side, pushing the right buttons to make it happen. Lucky boy. Lucky, lucky boy. But perhaps an unwise decision to make you a DI so young, aye?"

Marcus remained tight lipped and silent, determined not to play this man's mind games. If he waited long enough, Jackson would finally get to the point.

Perhaps sensing this, or perhaps getting bored by the lack of reply, Jackson pushed off the desk and stood directly in front of Marcus, invading Marcus's personal space. Marcus willed himself not to step back.

"We're taking over the case, as of now —"

"No, no way!" Marcus was vehemently shaking his head even before Jackson was finished his sentence. "I'm not accepting that —"

"We'll need complete access to all the files and reports, immediately."

Fury rose within him, unable to be contained. He jabbed his finger at Jackson, stepping up close, only just resisting the urge to grab him. "We have worked too hard, and too damn long on this case to step away now. You know these kind of cases take a long time to bring to arrests.. All I need is a few more weeks. You can give me that."

Hobson stepped closer, losing his nonchalance. But Jackson seemed only amused as he pushed Marcus' hand away. "You seem to be under the impression that this is up for negotiation." His eyes turned hard. "It isn't. You've got a dead witness who was under your protection. She was meant to be testifying in three weeks and bringing this whole damned operation down. You've cocked up badly, and now you're going to have to pay for that." He lightly slapped Marcus's cheek. "You're lucky you've not been demoted, so count your blessings, my son. Don't go expecting any more high-profile cases your way, though."

Angrily, Marcus shrugged off Jackson's hand. "I'm not letting this lie, you can mark my words," he bit out.

Jackson gave a shrug, unconcerned, then began to walk to the door, indicating Hobson to follow. "I expect all the files to be with me tomorrow. Don't try anything stupid."

With that, they walked out, leaving Marcus standing there, breathing hard, clenching his fists with the horrifying feeling that everything was being ripped away from under him... and he was powerless to stop it.

HE PULLED up outside their lodge and sat there in the car for a few minutes trying to muster the courage to go in. He had the strangest feeling of being detached from his body, as if he was floating above himself looking down in sympathy at this hollowed-out man who was wondering if he'd lost not only his job, but his wife also.

A heavy sigh escaped his lips, before Marcus climbed out and braced himself to go in. The air was quiet. Too quiet, as if it was holding its breath like he was.

"Soph? Where are you?" He called out as he walked into the deserted lounge. Resounding silence. Her car was outside, so he knew she was here. He continued to walk through, trepidation biting away at him, until he reached their bedroom and stopped at the doorway.

His breath stilled in his chest.

She sat there, on their bed that had always been witness to their love, her eyes surging with anger and bitter disappointment. The latter was by far the worse. He said the only thing he could think to say, his voice hoarse and low: "I'm sorry, *mo leannan.*"

Her tears dried. Sophia stood and moved towards him. "You think 'sorry' will be able to change any of this, bring Ella back, huh? No, it won't! Don't touch me!" She cried out, jerking away as he went to reach for her. That alone tore him up from the inside out. He froze as an icy hand crept between them.

"Please," Marcus quietly pleaded, "please don't let a woman who did nothing but hurt you and try to destroy you come between us now with her death. Otherwise, she still wins."

There was a moment of utter suspense as Sophia stared at him with disbelief and something unreadable in those dark pupils of hers. Perhaps pain, perhaps hurt. It had seemed the anger had burnt out, but what replaced it seemed more destructive.

"Whose tears do you think I cry for? For Ella, is that what you think? No, it's not only for Ella alone. It's for a woman still mourning her husband before we broke her heart into a thousand pieces as she watched her only daughter *die* right there in front of her, and we didn't stop it. We promised her, Marcus, *I* promised we would keep her daughter safe. And we broke it! *You* broke it! And now something is broken between us that I'm not sure we can get back. I trusted you... I trusted you, even though I vowed never to trust again," she whispered. Her chest was heaving, and the tears spilled freely over her cheeks. Sophia closed her eyes, then stepped back, far back. "You can sleep on the sofa tonight. I can't be with you. I can't look at you right now."

The door slammed shut on him, leaving him standing there, bracing the doorframe, his head bowed. He fought the overwhelming urge to let out a roar until his voice was hoarse and everything churning within him was forced out.

No sleep came for me that night. Every time I closed my eyes, my mind replayed over and over, like a horrifying film reel caught on a loop, the same scene again and again and again. The desperate look in Ella's eyes, the sound of the gun going off, the crushing weight of her on me, her crimson blood spilling over me that no matter how many times I scrubbed my body, I could still smell its metallic scent on my skin. I squeezed my eyes shut, hugging myself with my knees pressed up, only to frantically open them again as the nightmare returned.

So many times, I considered going to Marcus, knowing he would bring me comfort. But I had pushed him away to protect our marriage. If I went to him now, I would be using him, and as angry as I was with him, however right or wrong that anger was, I refused to do that. I loved him, even if I couldn't bear to be around him tonight. We'd only say dangerous, angry things, borne from our frustration and pain, that we wouldn't be able to take back.

Dawn weakly broke through, casting a pale light into the bedroom. I crawled out of bed, my head aching and tired, and walked over to the window, trying to find strength from the distant majestic mountain that never faltered. It knew its own beauty and importance, and that it would never be defeated by mankind. I really envied it right then.

For I knew what I had to do. The only choice left for me to finish this.

Alone, without Marcus.

I didn't want to do it. The thought made me break out in a cold sweat, my hands shaking.

We tried so hard, battled so long, and for what? Richard was still on the loose, Aneella was dead, and we still didn't know who the mastermind was, even now. Mr. Rogers and my mugging still kept me awake at night.

So, somehow, I had to find the courage and do what I'd been delaying.

I needed to become the bait.

[32]

The rain seeped down under my collar, soaking my t-shirt beneath, but I barely noticed as I hurried through the streets, head bent down.

I had agreed to meet him at the safest place I could think of: Saint Andrew's Cathedral. It was the church I had once walked into over a year ago when I first arrived at Aneella's. How that felt like a hundred lifetimes ago. If I'd known then what this year would bring, would I have stayed? I knew the answer without a murmur of hesitation. Yes, a hundred times yes. Forbidden, passionate love, as ours had been, opens the mind to new paths you would have never imagined in your heated dreams, and takes the very core of you and pushes it to the surface, until every inch of you is revealed and your soul is free. There was no going back from that.

But that didn't mean that there weren't consequences to pay for our actions. And we may have turned our forbidden love to a lawful one, yet still the price must be met. And my god, was I about to pay that in full.

I came to the heavy wooden doors leading into the

church and had to take a moment to catch some much-needed air, trying to steady my erratic breathing. My hand shook as I pushed the door open.

My footsteps echoed on the mosaic tiled floor as I walked across it. A yellow illumining glow from the side cloisters cast shadows over the pews. An elderly lady sat near the front, her head bent over in prayer. From the other side of the church, where the altar sat reverently above a three stained glass windows, a vicar dressed in robes walked across to light a candle. Otherwise, it was deserted, silent. Designed to bring peace and harmony.

If only that was so...

I discreetly checked my phone to see if he had tried to reach me. Nothing. Maybe I had missed spotting him. He was here, I could feel him. I ducked under one of the archways to the side of the main nave, slowly walking up it, casting my eyes everywhere. The vicar was extinguishing his lighter for the candles and gave me a friendly smile as I passed close by him. I pushed out a polite one in return, then picked up my pace to move away from him. It was best no one was near me right now. What could happen next was unpredictable, and therefore dangerous.

All at once, the hairs on the back of my neck stood up and a shiver moved down my spine.

I turned around slowly. He was standing there with that all-too-familiar cocky smile on his smooth cheeks, as if he didn't have a care in the world, as if the last time he saw me, I wasn't lying in a pool of blood caused by his hand. Like he had no need for forgiveness. I felt the nausea hit me, and a desire to run the hell away. But I forced it down.

"Richard."

.   .   .

MARCUS WENT into the office as normal, because he couldn't think what else to do. There was bound to be paperwork and calls to respond to. He would fight hard to get their case back, he would, with every fibre within him. But not today. Not today. His body and mind were weary and defeated, his heart sore. He had nothing left to give.

As he slumped in his chair, not even bothering to switch on the computer, Marcus pulled out his phone, hoping—even though he knew it was pointless—that Sophia had messaged him. He had called out her name through that firmly closed bedroom door. Silence had met him. Closing his eyes, he'd turned and walked out of their home, unable to bear it for one more agonising second.

He had never felt so achingly alone as he did right then, not even after Lucy had died. Sophia had reached a part so shockingly deep within him, she had forever claimed it as hers. There was no coming back from that. Did she even realise the power she had over him?

There was a soft tap on the door, then: "Sir?"

Marcus wearily raised his head, giving Jerry a vague smile that didn't reach his eyes.

Jerry waited a moment, then when nothing was uttered, he cleared his throat. "Any updates we should know about?"

Marcus turned away. "Aye, there is, but will you do me a favour and ask me again tomorrow?"

He could feel Jerry's gaze on him, reading between the lines of what Marcus had said as he was so strikingly good at doing. A still, silent minute. "I can do that. In the meantime, Libby, Tom's friend, is being moved into witness protection." Marcus looked up at Jerry, alert. "If we're going to let Tom say goodbye, it's got to be now."

"Then let's go," Marcus replied, standing up. "At least in this, we can get it right."

. . .

As I eyed him warily, everything in me locked up, as if to protect me.

Richard stepped closer, still that cocky smile on his face, though his face was thinner and his general appearance not as polished as he preferred. "What, no warm embrace or relief in seeing your husband... ah apologies, *ex*-husband, still in one piece? I had no idea I could be divorced without consenting to it. Guess it pays to have friends in high places."

He was trying to goad me, as he always did. Instead of immediately reacting with anger, I forced myself to wait a moment, before saying in a mild, even voice, "That's what happens when your husband tries to kill you: you're immediately granted a divorce with special dispensation."

That got a reaction, much to my surprise. "I wasn't trying to kill you, for god's sake!" Aware that he'd raised his voice, Richard forced it lower, but his voice was still vehement. "You fell onto the knife when your stupid current husband tried to grab me! So why the hell should I take the blame for that?"

I shook my head in utter disbelief. "You actually believe that, don't you? In your sick, twisted mind, you've excused yourself from any blame or wrongdoing, because God forbid you should ever take responsibility for your actions." I stepped up to him until we were eye to eye, any lingering fear I had now replaced by a churning disgust. "I always thought you were weak, that you had no backbone, no strength of character. But now, now I pity you. You want to know why?" I let a small smile grace my lips. "Because now, I know you are nothing but a coward who only brings himself humiliation and embarrassment. And I'm not afraid of you, Richard, for you will get what you deserve."

Richard suddenly grabbed me and pulled me towards a more sheltered alcove. I shoved him off. "Don't touch me," I hissed.

His eyes narrowed on me. "I'll tell you what I deserve, what I've wanted from the start: your damn programming codes and maybe a ready-made program into the bargain. Oh, and for good measure some cash. 10K should do it. For now."

I wanted to tell him where to shove his ludicrous demands, none of which I planned to give him. The words demanded to be let out. But I needed him to think I would give him what he wanted, if only to extract the information I needed.

"And what will I get in return?" I calmly replied, meeting him look for look.

Richard cocked an eyebrow, taken aback. Good. "My, my, my demure ex-wife has found some claws at last. Not quite the sweet and innocent now, are you, darling?" He drew a finger down my cheek, which made me shudder. "Wonder what your self-righteous police hubby would have to say about that? What is it that you could possibly want from me? I'm all ears."

A nerve ticked in my neck, but I prayed that was the only sign of my nervousness. I willed my voice to remain steady. "Two things. One, you give me the names of the masterminds behind this. I will give you three days to get away before I pass them on," I hurriedly added as he went to give a scathing retort, "and that's more than generous, wouldn't you say?"

A beat. "And the second?"

This was easier to say because I meant every damn word. "You will never come near me or Marcus again, nor will you make any more demands from us." I drew in a breath, every muscle in my body tense, and spat out, "Do we have a deal?"

There was a momentary flash of admiration in my ex's eyes as he contemplated me, playing me even now. It took everything I had not to look away.

"We have a deal, Sophia darling."

Relief mixed with apprehension flowed through me. How the hell was I going to do this? Had I bitten off more than I can chew? "Good... when do you want to do the exchange?"

"Tomorrow. I'll text you where to meet me."

"Excuse me?" I stared at him. That didn't give us very long to set up a trap. I had to think quick how to get longer. "How do you expect me to get the money by then?"

A hardness settled on his face, giving him a dangerous glint. "You think I'm waiting around any longer than that with a warrant on my head? You're lucky I'm giving you that long."

"Fine," I muttered, silently swearing. I couldn't push more on this without causing suspicion. "I'll be there."

Richard grinned. "Knew you'd see it my way."

At least I could tell Marcus, and hopefully he could act swiftly to arrange his undercover team to be there at our rendezvous.

To my relief, Richard went as if to move past me to leave... only to press up close to me, bend down, and whisper in my ear. "Oh, and because I don't trust you one bit, you'll be coming with me on the road for three days for collateral purposes-"

"The hell I am!" I protested wildly, fighting to push back from him.

"-before I give you those names you so desperately want." His hand gripped my arm, bruising my skin. I bit back a soft cry. "And just so we're clear, if you don't do this, then your poor unsuspecting husband will pay the price. I can guarantee my knife won't miss its mark next time. Afraid of me now?"

I stilled, a cold shiver slicing through me as if that steel blade was once more piercing skin, only this time the skin wasn't mine, but Marcus'. I closed my eyes with a shudder as a horrendous image of him bleeding in my arms burned my mind.

"How do you expect me to disappear for a few days without raising suspicion, or having him follow us?" I whispered in despair, knowing Marcus would not rest until he tracked me down.

"Well, now, that's down to you. But I would suggest you ensure he doesn't do that. You're good at leaving husbands for other men, so why not tell him you're having an affair. Hey, tell him it's me. How deliciously ironic that would be."

"How can you be so vile!" Hatred boiled within me as I spat the words out. "That would destroy him, and you know it."

With his other free hand, he cupped my hand in a tight hold, forcing me to look at him. "Exactly. But better his heart broken than his body, wouldn't you say, mmm?"

Richard held me prisoner for another moment. For one god-awful moment, I felt his stare on my mouth, and saw his head moving closer. Then, the sound of nearby footsteps forced him to let go of me and disappear, but not before he shot me a warning look. I let out a deep breath, rubbing my arm where it hurt. A choking sound in my throat threatened to escape, and I sunk down to the floor, holding myself.

It wouldn't just be Marcus' heart that I would be breaking to save his life.

It would be mine too.

[33]

Tom was dozing on the hospital bed, deliriously high on pain meds that worked like a treat to take the edge off. They'd put him in a private side room last night and he was very grateful, knowing his boss would have organised that. At least now he could catch some sleep away from the incessant noise of a busy hospital ward. How did people stand being here for months on end?

So, when a knock came at the door, he half-wanted to shout to come back later, if he had any energy, that was. Instead, he reluctantly opened his eyes and croaked, "Come in."

On seeing Marcus and Jerry walk in, Tom raised himself up, even as Marcus reached out a hand to stop him. "There's no need lad, stay as you are, aye."

Tom settled back down in relief. "Hi boss," he managed with a half, crooked smile. "Jerry."

Jerry gave a nod and smile from where he stayed by the door. "Good to see you looking a bit brighter there, Tom."

"Thanks... getting there. Be back soon."

Marcus came and sat on the chair near Tom's bed,

placing a hand briefly on Tom's shoulder. "There's no rush, believe me."

Hearing the ironic undertone, Tom looked intently at Marcus. "Has something happened? Did we catch the bastards?"

His boss dropped his head with a soft sigh, as if there was a crushing weight pressing down on his neck, like a hangman's noose. "Plenty of time for bringing you up to date when you're better."

Before Tom could reply, Marcus was straightening up. "Feel up to another visitor?"

"Who?"

"Libby."

Tom felt his heart lurch at the sound of her name and swallowed. She had been on his mind constantly, as he willed, hoped, dreamed, prayed she was alright.

Marcus watched him carefully. "I know you were keen to say goodbye. We thought you'd have more time, but she needs to be taken to her new home today for her own protection. I've got them to agree to let her come in. She's just outside the door." Seeing Tom sit up then, craning his neck to see her with a desperate need in his eyes, Marcus put a restraining hand on his arm. "But a few minutes only, understood? That's all I could get you."

Tom nodded. "Got it."

Marcus also nodded, standing up, paused then leaned down. "Tom, lad, make this as easy as you can for her sake... and for yours."

Tom felt his throat catch as he bobbed his head. As they walked to the door, he called out in a still weak voice. "Thank you. I... I appreciate you doing this for us."

They both gave him a small smile. Then, Marcus nodded to someone outside of the room before discreetly moving away. Someone walked in, and the door was quietly shut, leaving them alone.

Tom braced himself as much as he could, but seeing her standing there, alive and unharmed, still caused him to let out a relieved cry. "Thank God you're okay," he breathed out.

Libby, in sharp contrast, was staring at him in horror, twisting her hands together. "You're... you're really badly hurt..."

He tried to crack a smile, "It's not as bad as it looks. Lib, don't stand over there. Come here."

She hesitated, then to his immense relief, walked over to him, looking anxious and close to tears as she continued to gaze at his injuries. When she was finally within reach, he stilled her fidgeting hands with his, and squeezed them a little.

"Why did you do that, why go and face Jake by yourself?'

He looked deep into her eyes. "You know why." She looked so lost and distraught that it took everything in him not to pull her into his arms. He wanted to tell her he loved her, but he heeded Marcus' advice. "I would do it again in a heartbeat for my best friend."

He watched a tear roll down her cheek and could do nothing to stop it.

"Is that... is that all we are? Friends?" She raised her eyes to his, imploring him to deny this, tell her they could be more. Something wrenched inside him and all he could do was quietly say, "It's all we can be."

"No, no, it doesn't have to be!" Libby was grabbing his hand now, wiping away her tears with a sudden forceful-ness. "We can stay in touch, then you and me, yeah, when this is all over and the bastard is in jail, can be together. No one has cared about me like you have."

Tom had to close his eyes, unable to stand the hope in her eyes. "Lib, Libby." he slowly opened them, then reached out and cupped her cheek. "We won't ever see each other again, we can't. You're to be given a new identity, new life. I won't know where you are and," he rushed on as she tried to protest, "it's the way it has to be."

Libby was crying openly now, shaking her head. Unable to stand it any longer, he pulled her roughly against him, cradling her. "Shh, it's okay, it's going to be okay," he whispered into her hair. "You're gonna have a great life, a life filled with love and friendship and babies just like you dreamed about, away from here. You will, I swear it. Put this behind you, this life that's given you nothing but shit to deal with. You deserve more, you deserve everything."

The door was opening, Marcus was clearing his throat. Tom raised a hand without looking up, then gently pulled her tear-stained face to his. "Be free, Lib, and live every day, you hear me? You've been given a chance to start again. Don't waste it. Promise me, promise me, Lib."

Libby gazed at him, taking a heaving breath then nodded. "I promise."

Tom nodded too, "Good." He pressed his forehead against hers, his hand still on her cheek.

"I'm sorry." Marcus' voice was full of apology.

It was time. It took everything in him to slowly draw back and let her go one finger at a time. But somehow, he did it, and he held on to that encouraging smile, forcing down his own tears. That smile stayed on as she stepped farther and farther away until she reached Marcus, who nodded to Tom before gently leading Libby out of the room. It stayed until the door was shut and their shadows had moved away. Then it slipped, cracked, and broke. Only then did he allow the pent-up sobs to escape. He curled himself up into a ball and prayed for sleep to take him into oblivion.

I WASN'T aware of how I got home. I guess my body went into autopilot, because I found myself lying on our sofa, staring up at the ceiling and cursing my foolish stupidity as I forced back the tears. If I let them flow, I would completely fall apart and then we would all be destroyed.

Why did I think that I could control Richard? That for once, just once, I held all the cards in the palm of my hand? I may have won a small victory, but he would be the victor of the war, because he held to ransom everything I loved. He had all the power, and I none. All I could hope and pray was that afterwards, when Richard finally let me go, and I had the names of the masterminds to give to Marcus, that my husband would understand why I did what I did and forgive me. I was banking everything on his deep love for me at least stretching to that.

Oh, dear God, everything was moving too fast, too hastily. How could I face him tonight and lie to his face when we had been nothing but brutally honest with each other from the moment we first met? When should I break his heart by making him think I was leaving for good: straight away, or in the morning? Could I be selfish, for just a few more hours, and hold him as close as possible? He was already beaten down by what had happened to Ella, his fighting spirit low and vulnerable. The thought of kicking him at his lowest made me feel sick.

But he would be alive, he would live... and nothing was more important than that. At least for one glorious year, I had known what it was to love and be loved so completely, so thoroughly that not once had I questioned it. It would have to console me for the years ahead... if I made it out alive, of course.

There was the sound of tyres crunching on the gravel outside. A car door opening and shutting. Stirring me from my state of paralysis and drawing everything within me to stand up and do what I must.

MARCUS HAD BEEN PREPARING himself for an empty house, or worse a continued shut door. So, when he came in and saw Sophia standing there waiting for him, he felt everything in him leap with hope.

He hesitated for the briefest moment, then stepped across to her and softly kissed her on the cheek, which seemed a little damp. He felt her hands on his arms, squeezing him a little as if in pain, then let go. He searched her face, trying to read it. "I've missed you," he quietly said.

Sophia nodded, swallowed, then stepped away to the kitchen, lifting the kettle then putting it down again, as if confused by her own actions. That wall was still up, and he had no clue how the hell he was ever going to break it down. The thought sent him spiralling into panic.

The silence stretched on, not the comfortable kind. At a loss for words, he moved to put his coat down on the sofa where, only a few days ago, they'd made love. He felt her eyes on him, but when he turned to her, she was looking away, wiping down an already clean surface.

"How was today?"

Jolted by the question, Marcus felt a surge of relief. He

moved closer to where she stood, still not making eye contact with him, but at least wanting to engage.

"It was... tough. For Tom, at least," he replied.

"Why?"

Marcus moved so he was close behind her, watching her movements. "Today he had to say goodbye to Libby, you know, the girl he helped save by nearly costing his own life? She was going into a witness protection programme, so they won't see each other again."

Sophia spun around, her hand to her mouth as she stared at him.

"My heart breaks for the poor lad. He loves her, you see. Hey, now, don't cry," he murmured in concern, thumbing away tears falling down her cheek as she frantically shook her head. "Ach, you know I don't like it when you cry, *mo leannan*. He'll be okay."

"No, he won't," came the anguished whisper. "He won't."

"Sure, now, he will, you'll see." Marcus smoothed back her hair, kissing each of her cheeks. She pressed her head into his chest, clinging to his top. He gathered her close, holding her. She was beginning to soften against him, letting him in. Something within him healed a little, yet at the same time pushed hard at him to tell her he was off the case, at least for now. He had to do it now, while he was holding her to him, while her defences were finally down, and he had the courage. If they lost the trust, they would have nothing.

"Soph, Sophia, there's something I need to tell you. I-"

Before he could go any further, his words stilled on his tongue as her head swung up and she started pulling him towards the door by his hand, her eyes burning into him. "Come with me."

Marcus frowned, giving a little laugh of surprise, readily

accepting the reprieve he had been given even if he was completely flummoxed by this new wife before him. "Where?"

By now they were outside, and she had the most intense look on her face as she urged him along, their footsteps stirring up the leaves and birds around them. "To our loch."

She reached up and kissed him with a fire that made his body tingle, stopping him from asking anything else and do what she asked.

He followed her willingly.

THERE WAS a fever in my blood, a pulsing vibration through my veins as I urgently led him to our loch. Something beyond my normal, rational self had a grip on me and all I wanted, all I *needed* was to be one with him, to have him hard inside me, surrounding me, feasting on me, taking my soul as well as my body. *One night, let me have this one last night...*

Quickly, quickly I urged us on, feeling his questioning look on me even as his thumb tantalisingly stroked over my hand, sending small shivers down my skin.

The water seemed to be waiting for us, still and breathless. Stopping beside it, I turned to him, dragging his mouth down onto mine, hungry, demanding, my tongue seeking his. Marcus gave a soft groan as he opened to me, his tongue seeking mine, his hands pulling me tight against the length of him. I could feel his arousal pressed against me and was desperate to feel his bare skin. Yanking his jacket off his shoulders until it hit the ground with a thud, my hands flew to undo his shirt, almost ripping it in my haste. Catching my urgency, matching it, he helped me, dropping them both to the ground. I'm not sure which of us had his jeans and boxers off, but at last he was standing there beautifully naked, the sun glistening off his skin, his breathing heavy. I soaked it all in, trying to capture every part of him. My fingers reached out to trace over his chest, watching his muscles contract as I did, hear him give a small shudder before his hands cupped my face and took me into a deep kiss. My hands moved around to his back then moved down to his ass, my nails digging in.

"Take off my clothes, Marcus," I urged as his mouth left a hot trail down my neck. "Please, I don't want anything between us."

Marcus lifted his head to gaze at me. "You're different tonight," he breathed out, "you're burning me up here, that you are."

I couldn't say anything. Instead, I pressed harder against him, placing his hands on my hips. Slowly, tantalisingly, he moved his hands down me until he reached the hem of my dress, before moving them back up, only this time bringing the fabric up with him over my skin until at last I was free of it. Then I urged him on, even as he was kissing where my breasts were revealed above my bra, and his fingers were moving inside the rim of my knickers, teasing. Within moments, my bra and knickers were on the ground and at last we were both naked. A shaft of light glided over us, and Marcus stepped back, drinking in the sight of me, his eyes full of love and admiration.

"You're so beautiful, *mo leannan*," he said huskily. "You take my breath away. I'm sorry I don't tell you that enough. You should hear that at the start of every day."

My throat choked up, his words reaching a part of me that up until now had been untouched and barren. Right then, with him looking at me as he was, like he could hardly believe I was his, I felt beautiful, sexy, and worth loving. In this moment, I was being given everything, and selfishly, desperately I would take it all.

I moved up against him then, taking his face between my hands and into a hungry kiss. His mouth began its trail over my skin once again, only this time moving down until it reached my breast and enclosed over my nipple, making me arch my back and groan. His fingers found my wetness as they moved inside me and when my knees began to give way, we both fell onto the soft ground, me atop of him.

"I need to taste you," he muttered hoarsely, bringing me further and further up until his mouth was right between my legs and then taking me. I gasped as I stared down at us, my hands still on his face, my hair tumbling down over one side of my face. Within moments he was bringing me sweet release, I cried out his name. Before I could catch my breath, he moved up until he went inside me in one thrust, his hands on my hips, my breasts, in my hair as I sought out his mouth. Moving together, made to be each other's lovers, we both cried out as we took each other to the edge and over.

As I collapsed on Marcus, he put his arms around me. Lying against each other in the grass, my head on his shoulders and our legs wrapped around each other, I knew that it wasn't enough, that this passion between us would never burn out. Even now, my body hummed for him again.

Tomorrow was coming too fast, and my heart was already in agony. In a few hours, it would splinter and break. All I could do was pray our love was strong enough to survive, because if it wasn't, then this would be the last time he ever gazed at me with eyes full of love and wonder, or whisper against my hair, *"Tha gaol agam ort."*

[34]

There will come a moment in our lives when we're faced with a choice.

An impossible, soul-destroying choice.

But make it we must, even if it threatens to break us in half.

All we can do is pray that it's the right one.

Dear God and every angel listening,
*   let this be the right choice...*

[35]

Marcus awoke slowly, as if reluctant to face the day, even if his body remained sated and tingling from their lovemaking yesterday. Sophia had taken him into the shower with her before he could formalise everything weighing on his mind, and he was helpless to resist her even as his detective mind questioned what had changed for her to go from shutting him out to taking him inside her. She seemed reluctant to talk, using her mouth and body to drive all thoughts from him.

He hadn't been able to hold back the crippling tiredness after that and fell asleep though subconsciously fighting it with every breath. He was dimly aware that his wife paced around the room, her warmth no longer pressed against him. But it was like he was drugged, unable to drag himself awake enough to call her name.

Marcus sat up, rubbing his face and looking bleary-eyed around himself. Sophia was nowhere to be seen. He reached out to feel her side of the bed – it was cold. He pushed himself out of bed and hastily pulling on some boxers and jeans. He walked into the lounge.

It was then he saw the suitcase by the front door.

As he stared at it, then his wife as she slowly came out of the kitchen. A shard of ice cut into his heart so violently he swayed on his feet.

"What ... what is that suitcase doing there?" he stuttered as he felt the colour drain from his face.

ONE LOOK at his face and I nearly buckled beneath it, wanting to break down and tell him everything. One look, and already my heart was breaking, my throat choking up as waves of realisation hit him and he seemed to stagger back.

In fact, I stepped towards him before I was fully aware, only to stop abruptly as a flash of Richard's warning echoed loudly in my head. *"If you don't do this, then your poor, unsuspecting husband will pay the price. I can guarantee my knife won't miss its mark next time."*

"Soph? Answer me, please."

Deep breath, put on a mask, conceal every emotion.

Save him.

"I'm... I'm leaving you."

There, I'd said it, got it out. The hardest, cruellest, most untrue words I'd ever said. I closed my eyes, swallowing hard.

I heard his indrawn breath, his steps coming towards me, his hands gripping my arms as if to shake sense into me. "Look at me, Sophia!" Reluctantly I did, fighting hard to keep my face shuttered. "For the love of God, stop, and let's talk about this!" He pleaded with me, a desperate look in his eyes. "I know it's been a tough few days; I know you hold me responsible for Aneella's death, and I don't blame you. It's eating me alive knowing I failed to save her, you have to know that." His face creased with pain and self-loathing. It was taking everything I had not to reach out to him. "But don't give up on me, on us. We can-"

I couldn't bear it, and moved back forcing him to drop his hands, looking away. "It's too late, Marcus."

"No, no it's not! You promised me that last time you walked away, you would never run scared again. Do you remember?"

Of course, I remembered. I remembered every single word, touch, look between us. "That was before... before this. Before everything changed... Marcus, please-"

He cupped my face, closing the gap, cutting off my words, his eyes fierce on mine. "I know you love me, I feel it in every kiss and touch, in the way you look at me. Last night alone proves that. Don't deny it."

As if afraid I was about to, his mouth came down on mine, trying to draw a response from me. It took every willpower in me not to respond and open my lips to him, let him in. This was killing me and I'm not sure if I could stand another minute being with him like this and *lie*.

Somehow, I remained like stone and Marcus drew back, staring at me like I was some pretender acting as his wife. Which was exactly what I was.

He began shaking his head. "This isn't you, it isn't you...I don't know what the hell is going on, but I know you're not acting yourself. I'm not giving up on you, *mo leannan*, you're my life. I'll follow you anywhere, do anything. That's what love is to me."

He went to reach for me again and something desperate and unhinged gripped me, making me drop my barely held on facade. "You have to let me go, Marcus, you have to! I can't, I can't stay here...I...." The words started tripping out of me before I could stop them, and now I was gripping his bare chest. His hands immediately covered mine. "Don't

227

follow me, okay, please do this one thing for me so I know you're safe. Please, please!"

Now there was a frown deep on his forehead and he was staring hard at me as his detective instincts reacted and I knew I'd revealed too much. I bit back a sob, shaking my head even as he quietly but firmly said, "Has someone threatened you? Threatened me? Is that what's happened to make you do this?"

Too close, he was too close to the truth! Oh god... There was only one thing I could say now that would ensure he would let me go. The very thought of the words made me feel physically sick and I seethed with hatred towards the name I was about to say, forcing myself to look him directly in his eyes, as I said as coldly as I could, "I'm going back to Richard."

The deafening silence that accompanied this was the worst few minutes of my life. Marcus slowly pulled my hands off his chest as he turned a deathly shade of white. Then as if he couldn't bear to look, he turned his back on me. Tremors moved through his muscles.

"Then go... go, if that's what you want."

The defeated tone of his voice told me I had done exactly what I had to: turned him from me. This time he wouldn't come running after me when I walked out the door.

I knew I couldn't hold it in much longer. Allowing myself just one look at his beautiful, strong back, I picked up my suitcase and opened the front door, closed my eyes then walked out of our home, and away from the only safe haven I had ever known.

[36]

The sound of the door shutting sent a jolt of reaction screaming through his body, pain exploding everywhere.

He didn't know what to do, how to think, how to...

As if in stupor, Marcus staggered into the bedroom and lowered himself onto the bed. He dragged his hands through his hair, heaving silent sobs as he bent over, trying to keep the blind panic at bay, and failing.

Nothing made sense. Nothing! She couldn't love him like she had last night, as she had every day since they married and then leave him... for Richard. Her bastard of an ex. The man who had nearly killed her. Even saying that name had a rage building inside of him. She loathed Richard, she did, her nightmares were haunted by him. So why... why would she go back to him?

Think, dammit, think!

What had she said to him when her eyes had dilated in panic and... fear...

Come on, get your shit together, Marcus! Think, think!

Marcus began pacing, squeezing his temples as he cast

his mind back through the dense fog almost burying him right then. *Take me back, take me back to her words.*

Like a blast of light striking through the window, he heard them again as plain as day: *"Don't follow me... do this one thing for me so I know you're safe."*

Don't follow her, so he was safe. Safe. Which means she thought his life was in danger. Immediate danger. From-

Out of the corner of his eye, something caught in the ray of light coming through the dark clouds. It was Sophia's laptop that held all her programs. Why would she leave her laptop behind? She couldn't work without it. It never left her sight.

Acting on pure instinct, Marcus dove for it, then placed it on the bed, grabbing a t-shirt to shove on as he opened the laptop.

And there, stuck to the screen on a fluorescent pink post-it note, were the words:

Go to my inbox. Forgive me. I love you.

I DON'T KNOW how I managed to hold it together enough to drive away from Marcus. I think knowing the further away from him the safer he would be the only thing that got me turning the ignition key and pushing my foot down on the acceleration pedal.

I heard my phone go, alerting me to a text and felt my heart jump in anticipation. When I glanced over at it on the seat beside me, it flashed up Richard. I pulled over to the side of the road and opened it, my stomach lurching violently and my hands shaking a little. There was a location pin with a message.

Meet me here. Don't be late and don't do anything stupid. Bring the money and codes.

· · ·

I CLOSED MY EYES, breathing hard as waves of panic crashed over me. I was walking straight into my enemy's hands... and I was doing it with my eyes wide open. As far as insane, stupid decisions go, this one was right up there.

I can do this. I can do this.

THE LAPTOP WASN'T POWERING up fast enough, and Marcus was cursing it with every name under the sun. He started pacing just to stop himself from throwing it against the wall.

At last, it was on the login page, and in a flash, he was logging in as Sophia, using her password as the date the first time they had picnicked together by the loch – something only the two of them could know. With everything contained on this laptop, Sophia was ultra-careful and only shared it with him. Thank God she had.

The slow whirring of the laptop as it now loaded was enough to nearly have him pulling his hair out and wearing more of the floor out. When it finally reached the desktop page, he went immediately to the inbox. As emails came through, mostly spam, a few client ones, he scanned the inbox, looking at the recipients' names. Nothing out of the ordinary. Nothing that struck him as unusual. What had she wanted him to see?

Frustrated, Marcus dragged his fingers through his hair, looking up and closing his eyes. "Come on, *mo leannan*, help me here," he quietly pleaded.

Letting out a breath, Marcus lowered his gaze back to the screen.

And it was then he saw the sub folder titled *Slyfox*.

Immediately, he opened it up. There was a series of emails from unknown recipient, dated from about two months ago. Feeling something heavy thud in his stomach, Marcus opened the first one.

SUBJECT: You have to help me
   I'm sorry. There, I've said it.
   Now you will help me.
   Don't let me down.

AND THEN SOPHIA'S one line reply:
   What is it you want from me?

THERE WERE MORE emails following that, progressively got more threatening.

   When are you going to stop messing with me and give me
                  a time and place to meet.
   This isn't a game. Don't have a death on your conscience.

UNTIL THE LAST ONE, sent yesterday. The one that filled him with immense relief in finally understanding why she had done what she had done this morning ... and cold grappling horror striking him right through the heart.

   Bring the money and codes as agreed. You better not have told your husband the real reason you're leaving with me. If I discover you've set me up tomorrow at the meeting point,
      then you can watch me kill him and I'll enjoy every

moment of it. You stick to our deal of helping me escape and I won't need to touch his pretty face.

AND THEN HER REPLY.

I TOLD you I wouldn't, and I won't. You had better uphold your side with giving me the names of your bosses. You touch one hair on his head, you bastard, and I will become your worst enemy.

"OH SOPH, Soph, *mo leannan*... why didn't you come to me, ach?" he whispered.

Then he was grabbing his phone, taking a photo of the IP address, before instinct had him hiding the laptop in a drawer. He then sent the photo to Jerry before calling him.

"Yeah, it's me. Listen, I need you to run details and location from the IP email address I've just sent you... no, now! I don't care about anything else. It's Sophia, she's in-"

Marcus abruptly looked over towards the front door as a sound of tyres came from outside then an engine cutting.

"Jerry, I'll call you back. Get onto that for me."

Without waiting for a reply, Marcus hung up, raced to the door, and flung it open. "Soph..."

His voice died away as he took a staggering step back, his stunned mind trying to comprehend the truth staring him in the face.

An arm with a dragon tattoo reached out to strike him without warning.

. . .

"COME ON, work for me, you bastard!" I shouted at the satnav as it froze on the rerouting icon. It was a part of Inverness I didn't know, nor had ever wanted to—somewhere tourists never ventured into.

I was already seven minutes late, and the gripping fear that Richard would think I was not coming was sickeningly real. And if he didn't think I was...

In despair and frustration, I hit the satnav. By some miracle, it started working, and I put my foot down, only to have to slam the brakes when I saw that two cars up ahead had collided and were now blocking the road.

"Shit!"

I would have to abandon the car and go by foot. Parking it haphazardly on the side of the road, I grabbed my phone and bag and flew out of the car, barely remembering to shut the door, let alone lock it. Quickly, I shot out a text to Richard: 'I'm coming.'

Getting the map app up on my phone, I started running, passing the two drivers shouting at each other and into streets that looked as confusing as the next. The sky was heavy and dark, killing whatever sunlight weakly trying to get through. The buildings seemed to be closing in on me and the streets becoming narrower. It gave me flashbacks to the alleyway where I was mugged, and it took everything I had to keep moving forward. I rounded another corner, perspiring with the exertion and adrenaline pumping through me, my eyes constantly checking the map. It said I was two minutes away. No time to stop and catch breath.

One minute away. So close.

"You have reached your destination." Thank God.

Heaving hard, I flew around the last corner and skidded to a halt. Shadows cast their long arms over the alleyway, and I struggled to see, my eyes straining through the gloom.

I was alone.

"No, no, no!" I cried out, almost doubling over with the enormity. "No, please."

My moan of pain echoed off the walls. *I'd failed, I'd failed, I'd-*

"There's no need for the dramatics, Mrs. Armstrong. Really."

That voice, I knew that voice. Slowly, I turned until I came face to face with it. There stood Mr. Rogers, wearing the exact same suit he had worn when he questioned me about my program codes at his office in Glasgow, smiling blandly at me. And my world spun once more.

FOR THE TENTH time in about five minutes, Jerry tried calling Marcus, holding in his hand the IP address location and account holder. When he saw who it was registered to, he had to go and check, then check again. It didn't make sense, it couldn't be!

"Come on, pick up Marcus," he muttered as it rang and rang. Then came the answer phone message. Marcus always picked up, always. No matter what. So, if he wasn't, it meant something, or someone was stopping him.

With rising alarm, he tried calling Sophia, hoping like hell that maybe he was with her.

Once more it rang without reply, until it also went through to answer phone.

Something was wrong, very very wrong. He could feel it in his gut, and his gut never failed him.

Where the hell are you?!

Knowing it was futile, but unable to stop himself as he tried to stay calm and level-headed, Jerry pressed call against Marcus's name for the twelfth time.

Once more, it rang and rang and rang.

. . .

"WHAT... WHAT ARE YOU DOING HERE?" I stammered out, confused and disorientated. I whipped around. We were alone, as far as I could work out.

Mr. Rogers stepped forward with a slow, lingering look over my body that set me on edge. I wrapped my jacket more tightly around me.

"My, we do look flustered. Whatever is the rush?" he drawled.

"You haven't answered my question." There was an edge of anger to my voice now. I didn't have time for this. "Have you seen anyone else here since you arrived?"

Mr. Rogers paused, looking amused. "What's in your bag?"

I clutched it closer to me. "None of your business."

He stepped closer to me. "It's funny you should say that, because I think you'll find, Mrs. Armstrong, that it is very much my business."

That made me pause. A realisation grew within me. He was more involved than I had realised. Somehow, he was connected with this whole nightmare. I stared at him, my eyes narrowing in utter dislike and loathing.

"Ah, I see you are beginning to understand." He waved his hand around us. "You do seem to find yourself in dark alleyways rather a lot, don't you." It wasn't a question.

"I know you had something to do with my mugging," I said in a low tone. "You wanted my laptop ... and now I know why." Everything now was slotting into place. *How did we miss this?* Were we so blind? I raised my chin and looked him squarely in the eye. "You're in on this with Richard, aren't you? You want my programming codes."

There was a moment of stillness then Mr. Rogers gave a

slow clap. "Congratulations. Now you're showing some of that renowned intelligence," he drawled.

Trying to ignore the condescension, I pushed on, adrenaline rushing through me. "Where is Richard? Tell me right now." And when there was no answer, I stepped up close. *"Tell me!"*

There was a dangerous, knowing glint in his eyes. He gave me a cruel smile. "Perhaps it's time you went back home. Who knows who may have visited in your absence while I've been making merry conversation with you here?"

Sickening horror coursed through me. Marcus! They had played me, and like a fool, I'd fallen for it. I grabbed him by the arm, rage and fear coursing together. "You kept me here on purpose! If you've hurt Marcus in any way, I swear to God, I will kill you all!"

Mr. Rogers merely looked amused. "How sweet, your love for him." He leaned closer. "If I were you, I would start running. Time is running out. Can you hear that? Tick tock, tick tock."

His mocking laughter followed me as I turned and ran as if the hounds of hell were after me. Perhaps they were.

Marcus, my heart whispered in agony, Marcus...

Don't let me be too late.

[37]

Every minute was like a beating drum resounding loudly in my head.

Everything seemed against me, from the traffic crawling at almost standstill because of roadworks, to constant red lights and tourists ambling along in their cars coming out of Inverness as they enjoyed the Highland scenic delights. How I envied them and their easy, simplistic lives.

Finally, I was screeching into our drive, my tyres skidding on the gravel as I did. Marcus's car was still there, but there were tire tracks that were clearly not from either of us. Not even stopping to shut the car door, I sprinted up to the veranda. The front door was slightly ajar. Cautiously, I pushed the door open. Horror struck me as I surveyed the knocked over chair, the lounge rug bunched up. The signs of struggle were evident. Marcus hadn't gone easily.

Frantically, I searched every room hoping for something, anything that could give me a clue. Coming up with nothing, I fought back the waves of panic. Think, think!

I moved back into the lounge, trying to think back to what Mr. Rogers had said, any clue where they may have taken him. I still had what I wanted, so they would *want* me to come to wherever they had Marcus. They must have guessed that I wouldn't hand anything over to Richard if they haven't trusted him to meet me alone. That meant a lot was riding on this, too much for them to lose. They wouldn't stop pursuing us until we gave them these codes and the money, or one of us died.

So, I began to look again methodically, searching all the areas where our belongings had been disturbed. I went over to the door to see if it had been damaged or not, whether Marcus had willingly let them in thinking it was me, when I noticed a piece of paper pinned to the inside of the door. In my haste, I must have missed it earlier. There appeared to be writing on it.

Snatching it off the door, my urgent eyes quickly scanned the writing:

'IF YOU WANT to keep your husband alive, bring the codes and money to this location. Park the car, follow the path all the way to the top. Enjoy the climb. COME ALONE... or say goodbye to your darling Marcus. We will know. You are being watched.'

I DIDN'T KNOW what I was going to do when they realised that I had neither the money nor the codes, having purposely left the laptop in a safe place and praying like anything whoever had taken Marcus hadn't spotted it. Instead, I was betting everything on Marcus having a plan. He was always in control, at least when it mattered the most. If he was hurt—*no, don't think about that, Sophia.*

I toyed with the idea of calling Jerry, seeing his missed calls, but I believed every threatening word that I was being watched right now. So instead, I took a photo of the note, added the address to my map app, then left the note in an obvious place on the table in case Jerry came looking. I prayed to God that he would suspect something was amiss.

Then grabbing a water bottle, torch, jumper and first aid kit and stuffing it into a rucksack, I ran out of our home and jumped back into the car.

Every minute I wasn't with him, my head and heart felt like they were going to implode, paralysing me in absolute fear.

THE MUNRO MOUNTAIN loomed dark and foreboding as I stared up at it. I could barely see the top of it as mist and low cloud descended fast. It would be hard to see at the top, and the mountains were unpredictable and dangerous when the conditions deteriorated.

I squeezed my eyes shut, trying to steady myself. When I opened them, I noticed a dark figure coming towards me.

Richard.

Anger rose within me, and I made to storm over to him – only to still in terror when I saw something metal in his hands, and that manic look in his eyes. It looked like the same knife he had used on me. He came towards me, smirking.

I somehow found my voice, though I was unable to stop the tremor in it. "Why are you playing this ridiculous game of bringing me here? Bring Marcus to me, and I'll give you what you want."

He laughed. He actually threw back his head and laughed at me. The taunting sound echoed off the mountainside, shaking it.

"Oh, you think I'm the mastermind, even now! You think I'm running this show." Richard shook his head. "Oh, sweet Sophia, so naïve and stupid." He pointed the knife towards me, almost touching me with the point, before moving it to indicate the mountain behind us. "Better start climbing, darling, if you want to reach him in time. And don't worry, I'll be coming along behind, just to make sure you don't get lost on the hillside. That would never do, would it?"

THE COLD, sharp wind whipped against my numb cheeks, my eyes watered and my breathing became ragged. The jagged rocks beneath my feet were slippery and uneven, making me stumble and curse. My legs, aching from the frantic steep climb, moaned as I forced them on. My heartbeat far too fast, like the fluttering wings of an insect desperate to escape its trap.

I paused to grab a mouthful of water as I tried to gain back my breath. I had to keep going until there was no further to go and the light lost its battle against the gathering darkness. His life, and mine, rested solely on my shoulders.

I had come to an agonising realisation that I'd only ever felt strong with Marcus by my side. But for the first time since we'd met, I was truly alone, except for our enemies waiting for me. And these enemies wanted my code, my money, my blood. Nothing else would satisfy.

As if I'd conjured up his voice from my darkest terrors, the wind carried Richard's taunting words to me. "You better keep climbing if you want to reach him in time, dearest wife."

I spun round, trying to peer through the descending clouds as to how far away he was, how close on my heels he lurked. I could just make out the dim shadow of him and fear ripped through me.

I had no choice but to keep climbing, scrambling up the path for as long as it continued.

I would do anything to protect the man I loved.

[38]

My lungs were burning in protest, and my heart felt like it could pump right out of my chest, by the time I finally reached the pinnacle. The low cloud was clinging to my hair and face, and I struggled to see where the path carried on. I looked frantically around me, my adrenaline so high my hands were shaking.

There was that crunch of footsteps from behind me and I spun around and marched over to Richard, all fear gone as I grabbed him. "Where is he?"

He gave me that grin that once drew me to him but now rolled my stomach in loathing and nodded behind me.

I spun round, following his glance, seeing nothing at first. Then the cloud moved away... and there was Marcus, kneeling on the ground, his hands bound behind his back and a gag over his mouth. Everything in me lurched and collided.

"Marcus!" I rushed over to him, dropping to my knees before him and running my hands over his face, our desperate eyes colliding. "Are you hurt?" I whispered, the relief that I could touch him made tears run down my cheek. Marcus shook his head, even though I could see his eye was starting to swell. There was a burning, urgent look in his deep blue eyes as if he was trying to tell me something, indicating his head behind me. But I was too busy trying to undo his gag around his mouth, noting how tight his hands and feet were bound together and wondering how the hell I was going to get him free and both of us out of here alive. Marcus was powerless, completely vulnerable and my hope he could rescue us was gone.

But he was alive. And for that joy raced through me. I would fight till my last breath to keep him that way. I would find a way.

As my cold, wet fingers tried to undo the tightly knotted gag at the back of his head, Marcus was still trying to catch my attention and I at last looked directly into his urgent eyes, frowning as I tried to understand. "What?" I mouthed. Marcus's eyes widened in horror, and he tried to stand up, all the time fighting to speak while I tried to loosen the cloth.

Suddenly, I was being dragged backwards, my feet desperately scrambling on the rocky ground to stop myself. Panic came at me in a rush, clouding every other sense.

Then my eyes met my husband, who was moving his head up to indicate an action. It was enough for something important to click in me, and I remembered all the training he'd given me, on how to get myself out of a hold from behind. Taking a breath to compose myself, I then swung my head up to connect with my assailant's jaw with a crack, causing him to groan and loosen his grip enough for me to swing my elbow up into his throat and then stomach.

Richard let go of me completely, bent over in agony, and I raced back to Marcus, my hands more assured now as I loosened the gag. I could see the admiration in my husband's warm gaze and I smiled reassuringly at him, feeling stronger.

At last, the gag gave way, and I was able to push it down and off his mouth.

"Soph-" Marcus began, his voice husky and dry.

"I love you," I cut in, kissing him repeatedly. "I've never stopped loving you. I'm sorry."

"*Mo leannan*, don't you think I know that?" He managed to get out between my kisses. "*Tha gaol agam ort.*"

We pressed our heads together, as much for reassurance as for the chance to talk quietly.

"We need to get out of here." I whispered.

Marcus nodded, equally low as he said, "Do you think you can loosen my feet?"

"I think so. I-"

"Well, isn't this a touching scene?"

I knew that voice.

Everything in me froze, repelled, shock rippling down my body like a tide crashing over me. Marcus and I stared at each other in utter disbelief before slowly lifting our heads, carefully turning. It was as if we had stepped into a parallel universe that could take us under at any moment... for we came face to face with the one person who had nearly destroyed us with their death, yet now stood menacingly, a glint in her eye. And very much alive.

Aneella.

[39]

Aneella stepped closer to us as we stared up at her, unable to form any coherent words. The wind had whipped up again and stung our eyes. I could sense the clouds starting to roll back through.

"Isn't this quite the reunion party, mmm? Here we are again, the four of us." She crouched, with a smile that didn't quite reach her eyes, and took my chin in her hand. "Not quite as tete-a-tete as it was when it was the three of us, eh, Sophia darling? But we don't mind, do we, Richard?" She turned to look at him, still slightly doubled over as he grimaced at us. Aneella's eyes narrowed as she looked at him, before turning back to us. "I see you as sickeningly loved-up as ever, despite that little thing of being responsible for my death. God, what does it take to break you two up?"

"How..." I managed to get out.

"How am I alive?" She cocked her eyebrows, letting go of my chin. "How indeed."

Marcus leaned closer to me, so we were a breath from each other, as he looked Aneella with growing understanding and carefully replied, "Everything makes sense now, why I was denied seeing your body, then taken off the case. You could only have achieved this with someone on the inside, right?"

She gave him a long look that embodied powerful self-confidence. "Everyone can be bought for the price of gold... everyone."

There was a sickening realisation hitting Marcus as he slowly said, his words almost lost over the wind. "You have the doctor on your books, doing your bidding, the Glasgow police...." He paused, then said in horror, "You've been the mastermind all this time."

I stared at her, shockwaves leaving me speechless. Of course, of course she was... How did I miss this, how did I not guess? Richard didn't have the brains or cunning for this kind of operation. But she did, oh, she did.

Aneela gave a mocking bow. "Never suspected me, did you? All this time you thought I was some lovesick girl doing anything for her lover, when the truth was, he was working for me."

Marcus gave a faint smile. "Aye, you played us all, acting the part to the hilt, determined to bring us down while creating the perfect scenario of being 'dead' so no one would be watching you. Well played, Ms. Blair, well played."

Aneella gave a smile in return that was as deadly as a snake's bite. "Don't worry, dear detective, it's not your fault you refuse to see the betrayal in those you trust. It's quite sweet, really, and why you two are just tickety-boo perfect for each other." She turned her cutting gaze to me. "Charming isn't it, having your best friend, ex-husband and current husband all together like this? If only we'd brought some champagne to toast our imminent business deal before we all bid each other," she smirked. "...farewell."

The menace with which she spoke that last word raked shivers down my spine.

The cloud thickened around us again, and I almost lost sight of Richard, who was now straightened up behind Aneella. I needed to keep Aneella talking, as I saw out of the corner of my eye Marcus trying to loosen his hands from the rope binding them. So, I pounced on the one thing I knew would make her pause, perhaps stumble. I didn't have to dig very deep to find the right level of anger.

"And what about your mum? My god, Ella, she thinks you're dead! You know she collapsed when she heard the news about you, not more than *six* hours after burying your dad!" I rose to my feet, forcing her a step back from Marcus, the wind almost knocking us off our feet. "Are you so callous that you don't even care about your mum now? Have you no conscience at all?"

I had hit a nerve. I could see it in the way her eyes shifted away from me and the fluttering in her throat. "My mother is of no importance to you."

I stared at her. "No importance?" I laughed hysterically. "You're right. You were not the one who held her when she broke into a thousand pieces, you were not the one who had to witness her losing the will to carry on. You are not the one who watched her daughter be 'shot' right after burying her husband. You weren't the one who thought she was responsible for your death. So don't you dare tell me she's of no importance to me!" I shook my head, fighting back pent-up tears. "You do not deserve her."

Aneella's eyes narrowed. "You always did want to be the perfect replacement daughter for her. It used to make me sick the way you would suck up to her, trying to make her love you, to replace me. You make my skin crawl with your need for love and acceptance, and how easy you are to manipulate."

"At least I do love her," I shot back, "something I don't think you're capable of doing. You're nothing but a cold, heartless bitch." I couldn't stop these next words from slipping out. "Your mum would be better off if you were dead-"

The resounding slap across my face shocked me more than any words she could have said, and I knew I had pushed her too far. "Enough!" she screamed in my face. "I'm sick of looking at both of you. Give me what I asked for!"

Before I could react, she was tearing my rucksack off my back and ripping the zip open, emptying the mundane contents onto the ground. I turned to Marcus, and we held each other steady as we prepared for the explosion to come. Still, when the rage erupted, it seemed to rock the very earth beneath us, the mountain quivering in protest.

"Where are my goddamn codes and money?" Aneella leaned over us, casting a long, dark shadow, her eyes spitting with uncontrolled fury.

We remained silent. Richard stepped closer to Aneella, watching her as warily as we did. Every sense in me was on full alert. Marcus leaned a little closer to me from behind to whisper in my ear. "I saw others here."

I gave the faintest nod. I had realised that it wasn't just the four of us here on this precarious pinnacle. But through the mist gathering it was impossible to see more than a few feet in front of us. Every nerve in my body was on edge, as I frantically tried to think.

"I said, where are my codes?"

Aneella grabbed Marcus's hair, yanking him towards her, dragging him along the ground, kicking him in the ribs as she did. Marcus bit back a howl. I launched myself at her, clenching my hand around her arm to try and force her to let go, as I screamed at the top of my lungs, "It's me, it's me that didn't bring them, so take it out on me, not him!"

She seemed too far gone to hear my pleas, yet something must have penetrated for she abruptly let go of Marcus, to my sobbing relief. I immediately pulled him back up to kneeling from where she had left him sprawling on the stony ground and used my body to protect him as he took heaving gasps of air, spreading my arms wide.

Aneella whirled around after letting go of Marcus. I had no idea who or what was coming, with her back turned to us, but every muscle in me was pulled painfully tight. I could see Richard staring at Aneella as if he hardly recognised her. No doubt, up until now, she had kept that dangerous rage under control. But he must have known it was there, as I had. The wind picked up speed and seemed to whirl her around as she turned back to us, her prey caught up in her dangerous game.

Her hand reached into her pocket and, far too slow to react, I found myself staring down the barrel of a gun.

The cold reality was different than anything I had seen in a movie. I felt my body slide out of itself as if it refused to believe what was happening. My head was rushing, my breath quickening. I could no longer recognise the difference between the wind and the rushing in my ears. Dimly, I was aware of Marcus shouting as he frantically tried to get out of his ropes, of Aneella screaming words as she came up close and pressed the gun on me, of a figure in the mist running towards us. My only point of reality was the coldness of the barrel pressing painfully against my forehead and that strange resignation that these may well have been my final few breaths on this earth. I couldn't even cry out, though my heart wept in broken despair.

I wasn't ready to die.

My shaking hand reached behind me to find Marcus,

stilling him in his desperate struggles, touching him one last time.

Then I slowly closed my eyes, unable to bear looking at the undiluted hatred in the face before me that I had once adored. Instead, I kept my hand on the man I loved with my entire being, pictured him in my mind, and waited for the deadly shot to come.

It never came.

There was frantic sound of struggle, then the feel of the cold steel suddenly left me. I heard a shout of "No!" My eyes flew open, only to see nothing but the unmistakable back of my ex-husband standing in front of me... as if protecting me. Aneella was scrambling back to her feet as if she had been pushed over. Marcus, who had been leaning towards me as if trying to do the same thing, urgently said into my ear, "Quick, grab the gun!" He indicated where it lay on the ground only a few feet from us.

I flung myself towards it, my fingers almost, almost grasping it. I was so focused on getting it, I didn't see the kick to my stomach. Then I was doubled over in searing pain, gasping for breath, as Aneella grabbed the gun. Marcus's voice rang out loud: "Don't you touch her!" Richard once more came between me and Aneella.

"For god's sake, stop Ella!" Richard exploded. "What the hell is wrong with you! We never agreed to this—where did you get the gun?"

Aneella gave a humourless laugh as she stood there with her legs braced. "You're really asking me that? Why do you suddenly care so much about her? Thought you would be glad to finally be rid of her. She's never going to give us what we want, so why the hell does she get to have her happily ever after, when we don't?"

Richard stepped closer to her, his voice turning smooth and crooning, "Darling, we'll get our happily ever after.

When have I ever let you down, mmm? It'll be you and me like we always planned." He reached out and cradled her face, then continued in a whisper to her that Marcus and I couldn't catch.

I was still struggling to catch my breath, even as my stomach wanted to heave up everything in it. A calming hand came down on my back, and I managed to turn my head to the side. Marcus had somehow managed to loosen his hands from the ties and now was hovering like a protective shelter over me. He hadn't had time to undo his feet, too desperate to reach me. "It's okay, *mo leannan,* you're okay, lass, deep breaths." he murmured. I nodded, obeying him before we turned warily to Richard and Aneella.

Richard was pulling her closer towards him again and she seemed to be yielding. I knew Marcus was biding his time as to when we could try and escape while they were distracted by each other. From the corner of my eye, I could see he had almost managed to get his feet loose. Any minute now...

Aneella shoved Richard away. He stumbled and fell backwards onto the hard ground, almost landing on top of me and Marcus. She stalked towards us, the wind whipping her hair and coat around her like dark, fallen angel wings. "Enough, I'm sick of you and your smooth-talking bullshit. I don't need you anymore." She raised the gun again, once more aiming dead point for me, though her way was now blocked by my ex. "Just like she's of no use to me now. Not that she ever was, the clinging limpet who sucked the life out of me." A cold, triumphant laugh erupted out of her. "I can hardly be prosecuted for it now can I, seeing as I'm technically dead. Isn't that right, detective?"

The question was aimed at Marcus, who quietly, calmly said even though every tendon on his neck was beating wildly. "You need to lower the gun, Aneella. Even the dead can face charges."

Her eyes narrowed, before she turned back to Richard, dismissing Marcus, her voice pounding the air *"Get out of my way!"*

Everything stilled, as if suspended in time. I was out of ideas, out of thoughts, my body and heart buffeted and drained. Here I sat between a man I had innocently loved as a young girl and woman, and the man I now loved as a woman with everything I had within me. It was almost unbelievable that I would find myself in this place as my last resting place.

It was abundantly clear, as we stood on this mountain, that Aneella had stepped over the edge of rational and become manic. Richard turned to look at me, really look at me, as if seeing me clearly for the first time. He took in my pale face, the tears threatening to spill, yet stubbornly being held back, the steely courage he had never seen, the light that had been awoken in me by another man, my unwavering gaze. And it was like something altered within him, a sagging realisation, a contrite and guilty awareness hovering over him.

He nodded, closed his eyes, then turned back to Aneella to quietly say, "I can't let you kill her. She deserves to live."

Aneella stared at him. "You're protecting her! Her, the woman you claimed to loathe. How sweet and totally humorous that is." She let out the maniacal laugh that I had come to fear.

Richard held her gaze, while I stared, flabbergasted, at his back, hardly daring to believe that this was the man I had thought hated me. "Looks like I am, so you're going to have to get through me to reach her."

Silence. Even the wind stilled. My lips moved in fevered prayer.

Aneella cocked her head, gave a nonchalant shrug. Then, without a flicker of emotion, she said, "So be it, darling."

The loud, echoing crack of the gun made the birds erupt in protest. Richard slumped sideways onto the ground, blood pouring out, his eyes wide and staring, as if he too could scarcely believe she had pulled the trigger.

Then I was screaming Richard's name, scrambling over to him. Marcus leaned over him to listen for his breath. With solemn eyes, he shook his head softly at desperate, despairing me. Richard was dead. My first love, my first husband, then my sworn enemy, now sacrificing his life to save mine.

"No," I moaned, drawing a still warm but lifeless Richard to me. No, no, none of this was right. He hadn't deserved to die, only to serve time for his crime. This couldn't be happening... I turned to Aneella, who still stood over us, seemingly unaffected, and cried out in anger and aghast, *"What have you done?"*

She gave a careless shrug that made me want to heave in sickening understanding of how little she cared. "He told me to. It was easier than I thought to pull the trigger. Would you look at that."

I shook my head. What had happened to the vicarious, life-loving girl we had all been swept up by? "I thought you loved him. Isn't that why you pursued him even though he was with me, why you weaved this whole damn web of deception and lies, so you could have him and my money?"

Aneella gave an incredulous laugh. "Love? Love makes you weak and pathetic, look at you! Always trying to protect, first Richard, now this detective. No, I'm glad to be rid of him, to be free of his disgusting clinging." Then she leaned dangerously towards me and said icily, "Now it's time for me to dispose of you, sweet Sophia."

Before I could react, Marcus was shoving me down, then launching himself at Aneella, and they both fell to the ground.

I scrambled up, flinging myself towards them, my hand frantically trying to find anything I could use as a weapon. A rock, I had a rock clasped in my hand. They were rolling and Aneella was fighting like a wild animal. If I could just knock her out when the back of her head was towards me-

Now! My hand rose and went to swing out.

Only it never reached its target.

Instead, a sudden agonising pain to the back of my own head had me screaming out... before heavy darkness descended.

[40]

The world had become a confusing mass of moving images that made no sense. Voices drifted in and out, but I couldn't seem to make sense of the words.

Why was it so hard beneath me? Something sharp was cutting into my face, yet I seemed unable to lift my head away from it, as if my limbs had sunk into the ground.

I tried to open my eyes. Blurring faces were there before me. Why was everything so misty and dim? Two dark things came towards me, leaning down. Instinctively, I closed my eyes again.

As if from a long way away, as if I was once again under the loch water, sinking deeper and deeper, a voice said, "What shall we do with her?"

That voice... so familiar... I...

Then, "Leave her here. She won't last the night, and they'll think she killed him."

Everything blurred again, coming in and out, distorting, buzzing, before,

"What about the other one?"

A small part of me that was still functioning, fought to catch those next words. Had to hear, I had to remember-

"Oh, he's coming with us, darling. He's our collateral."

The world turned dark and depthless again, as the voices drifted away...

[41]

It was the cold, whipping rain that brought me around, as it covered me like a wet blanket and the ground beneath where I lay, bringing me determinedly back from the unconscious. Or perhaps it was my will to survive dragging me into the living again, refusing to allow me to simply give up and die here on the mountaintop. Or maybe the mountain itself was trying to save me, as it had done once before when I had been broken inside.

Shivering, I became aware that my mouth was full of grass and dirt from where I lay facedown on the ground. Slowly, I raised myself up onto my knees, unable to stop the groan slipping out when blinding pain ripped through me. I reached back to touch my head, then brought my hand back around. Blood coated it. Nausea hit me hard, and I bent over and retched.

As I took deep breaths, whipping the stinging tears from my eyes, I turned my head sideways. Richard's body still lay there as before, as if frozen forever.

I had to turn away, unable to bear looking at him.

Everything was coming back to me, Aneella, the gun, the voices, the fight, the blinding pain, Marcus—

Oh God! Forcing myself up to my feet, I looked frantically around. Let him be here, let him be —

I stoodalone, no other living human with me, as if Marcus and Aneella had never been.

Blinding, searing panic surged through me. No, no, no, he couldn't be gone! What had they said? Think, Sophia, think! They said, they said—

"Oh, he's coming with us darling. He's our collateral."

She had him, she had him.

Still, I kept looking around, the mountain spinning with me as I denied the glaring truth that they had taken him... until, exhausted, I lifted my head up to the skies raging in unison with me, and screamed at the top of my lungs,

"Marcus!"

[42]

I will find you; I swear to God that I will. No matter what it takes, no matter how long, I vow with every breath within me that I won't give up, I won't back down in fear.

She is not going to win, not again. She is going to pay for what she's done. She will not rob us of our future, I won't allow it.

You've taught me to be strong, courageous, to be fearless. That I'm worthy of being loved, every part of me, the ugly parts as well as the good. You have given me that, my lover, my best friend, my heart and soul.

I will take every part of our love and I will use it to find you. Because you are alive: I know it, I *feel* it. Your heart still beats strong. You won't give in. You will fight to your last breath to get back to me.

I can sense you in me, binding us together.

I'm coming, I promise, my Scottish warrior. Don't stop fighting. Stay alive.

The darkness may have touched us, it may be trying to destroy us.

But it will not win. This I vow right now, right here.
I love you. I'm coming, Marcus.
Don't you dare give up on me.

To Be Continued....

ACKNOWLEDGMENTS

So many people to thank and I'm incredibly grateful for every single one of you.

First of all, thank you to my amazing family for supporting me every step of the way. Thank you to my daughter, Emily, for coming up with so many fabulous plot ideas, for reading through and editing my book, for encouraging your friends to read my book and generally being awesome. Thank you to my son Luke for encouraging me so much and ensuring I didn't get too distracted by other things when I'm meant to be writing! Thank you to my husband, Nigel for your praise and encouragement, and for being relaxed about me working part time so I can write during the rest of the time.

Thank you to my mum and dad, Ken and Sandy, for being such a supporter to me. And to the rest of my family for being there for me. This book is for my mum in law, Rosemary, who recently passed away. We miss you. You loved nothing more than sitting and reading, so this book is dedicated to you.

Thank you to my amazing publishing team at Gen Z Publishing, especially Lisa, Morissa, China, and Shannon. I'm so grateful that you took a chance on me with publishing my first book *Those We Trust* and encouraging and supporting me every step of the way since. Here's to many more years together working as a team.

Thank you x 1 million to all my readers and friends, who have brought my books, written incredible reviews and eagerly encouraged me to get this book written because you needed to know what happened to Marcus and Sophia. I really hope you love this book as much as I loved writing it. Special shout out to Betsy, and Pattie, my biggest number one fans! This book is for you.

Thank you also to my fantastic friends all around the world with your love, support and enthusiasm. It means far more than you will ever know.

Lastly, please do join my writing community at www.mariejonesbritishwriter.com.
And most of all, enjoy *Those We Seek* as we carry on the story of Marcus and Sophia.
The final book in the trilogy is coming soon. Stay tuned x

www.ingramcontent.com/pod-product-compliance
Lightning Source LLC
Chambersburg PA
CBHW030634030726
47497CB00006B/1789